Death
AT THEIR HEELS

by MARGARET GOFF CLARK

Cover by John Floherty, Jr.

Scholastic Book Services

New York   Toronto   London   Auckland   Sydney

Acknowledgment

The author wishes to thank Ronald G. Tozer, Interpretive Services Supervisor, Ontario Ministry of Natural Resources, for his generous help in giving information on Algonquin Park and checking the manuscript.

For the one with whom I share canoe and tent, my husband, Charles.

Another book by Margaret Goff Clark
available from Scholastic

Mystery Horse

Contents

Phone Call at Night

The ring of the phone cut through the roar of a speeding car and gunfire.

Denny Mitchell slid deeper into the big chair in front of the TV. Nobody would be calling him.

The phone fell silent after the second ring. Rick had taken the call upstairs.

Denny stared at the fast action on the TV without seeing it. That would be Rick's girl friend, Beth, on the phone. Rick talked to her for at least an hour every night. He might not even come downstairs before he went to bed.

And I thought it would be so great to have a brother! Denny leaned his head in his hands and stared at the rug through a fringe of sand-colored hair. He remembered his mother's happy glow as she told him, "When Vince and I get married you'll have a brother. You'll like Rick. He's seventeen, just four years older than you."

His mother was right. Vince's son Rick was just the kind of brother he'd have picked for himself. He was an outdoorsman, tall and well built and good at sports. Yet, he could sit down with a book.

Denny liked and admired him at once. The only trouble was, Rick didn't seem to like him.

Mom had married dark, handsome Vince Baline on July tenth, but they had decided to put off their wedding trip for a month until Rick's summer job was finished. She said that would give the two boys time to get acquainted before they were left on their own.

It had been a dismal month for Denny. His mother floated in a happy daze as they moved into Vince's comfortable house in a Buffalo, New York, suburb. But even before he had his suitcase unpacked, Denny was lonely for his friends back in Cleveland where he had lived all his life.

He would have turned to his new stepbrother for companionship but Rick ignored him. If he wasn't at work he was out with his friends or up in his room. When he was with Denny, he acted as if he were putting up with him because he had no choice.

Now that the boys' parents had left on their delayed honeymoon, Denny felt lost. At least when Vince was here he had talked to him about school and Denny's hobby of photography. Rick never seemed to have anything to say.

A slight noise in the hall doorway made Denny twist around in his chair. Rick, tall and dark haired like his father, was standing just inside the living room. His gym shoes had made no sound on the carpeted stairs.

Denny looked at Rick's face, hoping as always for a friendly expression. What he saw shocked him. In spite of his tan, Rick was pale and his eyes were as blank as the stone eyes of a Greek statue.

"What's the matter?" asked Denny. "Are you sick?"

Rick crossed the room like a sleepwalker and came to a halt in front of the cold fireplace. He kicked at the firescreen with his toe.

Finally he said, "No. I'm all right."

"You don't look all right."

Rick continued to stare at the hearth. "Turn off that blasted TV."

Denny obeyed. In the silence that followed he heard Aunt Wilma's cat crying to get in next door. A moment later a car rushed by on the street in front of the house.

Rick faced the room but his eyes still had the vacant look. "I'm getting sick of hanging around here. How about you?"

"It's for the birds," Denny agreed. He was surprised at the man-to-man question. Rick generally talked to him as if he were a kid.

"Uh, I was thinking of something we could do." Rick drew a deep breath and this time he looked directly at Denny. "How'd you like to go camping?"

"Camping! Do you mean it?" In his wildest dreams Denny had never dared hope for anything that good. He had always wanted to go camping but he had never had a chance. There hadn't been a Scout troop in the area where he had lived in Cleveland, and his grandfather wouldn't take him camping. He had said he was too old to sleep outdoors.

"Yeah, I mean it," said Rick. "We'll take a tent, sleeping bags, the works." His expression was deadpan.

Denny couldn't believe his luck. Rick acted bored when he had to drive Denny as far as the swimming pool in the park. He wouldn't even play gin rummy with his new stepbrother in the evening. Why all at once would he want to take him on a camping trip when there'd be just the two of them? Maybe it had something to do with that phone call.

"Who was that on the phone?" asked Denny. "It wasn't Beth, was it?" Rick usually talked a long time to his girl.

"No, it wasn't Beth and it wasn't any of your business," snapped Rick. "Now are you going camping or am I leaving you with Aunt Wilma?"

Denny was startled by Rick's tone of voice. His stepbrother ignored him most of the time, but he had always been polite.

"I'm going," Denny said promptly. "When are we leaving?"

"Tonight. As soon as we can get ready."

Again Denny was surprised. From what he had heard, people started on camping trips in the morning, or at least in daylight.

"Won't it be hard to pitch a tent in the dark?" he asked.

Rick frowned. "By the time we get where we're going it won't be dark. It'll be morning. You're as finicky as Aunt Wilma."

"Oh, man!" exclaimed Denny. "What's Aunt Wilma going to say?" She was Rick's aunt, but she had said that now Denny was part of the family he should call her Aunt Wilma, too.

Rick was silent for a moment. Then he said, "That's one reason we're going tonight, so we don't have to argue with her about going away."

Denny stared at him, wishing he could see into his mind. He was sure Rick had forgotten all about Aunt Wilma. That business about leaving tonight because of her, he had dreamed that up just now. His stepbrother had some other reason for leaving in such a hurry. How could he forget his Aunt Wilma when she lived next door and had been popping in here every hour since Mom and Vince had left for Bermuda three days ago? Something big must have come up to make him forget Aunt Wilma. But what?

During the past month Denny had discovered Rick had his moods. Sometimes he seemed to close himself up into his own mind. Then you could talk to him and he wouldn't hear.

"He's in love," Vince had said. "You have to let a person be a little foggy when he falls in love. I've been out in orbit myself ever since I found your mother."

But Denny was quite sure Rick wasn't thinking about Beth right now. He acted as if something had scared him.

Denny said hesitantly, "What's up, Rick? You act — funny."

Rick gave a sigh. "What an imagination you have! Here are the simple facts. My job's finished for the summer and I want to go off and take it easy for a while. We don't have enough cash for motels or a lot of gas, so why not go camping?"

"OK," said Denny. "I'm with you." He wasn't convinced by Rick's explanation, but he wasn't going to argue about it. It would be a lot more fun to go camping than to hang around the house until school opened.

Rick started across the room. "Come on. Let's go up to the attic and get our gear." Halfway to the hall door he stepped back and pulled the drapes across the picture window at the end of the living room.

Now why did he do that? wondered Denny. Rick never closed those drapes. No one did. Who did Rick think was going to look in that window? Outside was a sheltered garden surrounded by high shrubs and edged with pine trees. Vince had even rigged a spotlight out there so they could look out the window and enjoy the garden at night.

Vince loved flowers. He said he inherited his interest in gardening from his Hungarian ancestors. "Baline is Hungarian for Valentine," he had told Denny.

"One reason I bought this place outside of town was so we could have some land of our own," Vince had remarked one day last week. "You know, Rick and I lived for a while in a little apartment in downtown Buffalo. That was a couple of years ago, right after my divorce. Before that we had a house in Cleveland. My former wife still lives there — with her new husband."

Vince had paced back and forth looking unhappy as he always did when he spoke of his first wife.

"Rick and I got tired of that little apartment," he went on. "It was no place to bring up a boy in the heart of the city like that, and I was glad when my sister Wilma told me this house was for sale. Here we get some elbow room and green grass and flowers and my little vegetable garden."

Denny decided to say nothing about the closed drapes. Rick would probably explain that was to keep Aunt Wilma from peeking in. And that would be another lie because Rick's Aunt Wilma wasn't the peeking type. She'd open the door and walk in if she thought she was missing something.

As if he were thinking the same thing, Rick detoured to the front door and snapped on the lock. Then without a word or look, he went up the stairs two at a time.

The attic was not crowded. Though Vince and Rick had lived in the house for over a year it was plain to see they hadn't collected much junk.

Rick glanced around the attic. "We have all the camping stuff we'll need and it's only been used once. Dad and I bought it new last summer before we went to Algonquin Park." Rick lifted a bulging packsack. "Here we are. You bring the other pack. Take it in my room."

Denny had heard about the trip to Algonquin, the big park in Canada where Vince and Rick had paddled from one lake to another and had pitched their tent all alone on an island. How great to have a father to take you camping! he had thought. His own father had died when he was seven.

The packsack was heavy so Denny dragged it into Rick's room by a strap.

9

Rick was wrapping a faded shirt around a pair of binoculars. He stuffed the bundle into his packsack before he asked, "You too weak to carry that pack?"

Denny felt hurt. "No sense carrying it if I can drag it, is there?"

Rick shrugged. "Get yourself some clothes and put them in the pack. Then bring it down to the kitchen and don't drag it down the stairs."

"How long are we staying?" asked Denny.

"I don't know. Till we get ready to come home."

"School starts in three weeks. But I wouldn't mind being late by a few days." Denny grinned. "Or a couple of months."

Rick did not look amused. "We'll be back before school starts. This is my last year and I'm looking forward to it."

"Mom and Vince will be home in a week and a half," Denny reminded him.

"So? We'll call them up." Rick rummaged in his dresser for underwear and socks. "Get a move on."

When Denny reached the kitchen, Rick was already raiding the shelves for easy-to-carry food.

"If we like dehydrated soup three times a

day we're all set," commented Rick. "Dad really stocked up on this stuff. Before you and Sara joined the family we used to eat a lot of soup and TV dinners. Ugh!" He made a face that expressed his opinion of instant meals. "Your mother's the best thing that ever happened to us. And not just because she can cook." He went on packing, dumping dried milk into one plastic bag and oatmeal into another.

Denny sat on the kitchen stool and watched Rick stow the food in a thermal bag.

"We can hang that bag of food on a rope over a limb," he remarked. "I read about that in a book on camping. Keeps it out of reach of the raccoons."

"Or bears," added Rick.

"Bears! Where are we going?"

"Algonquin Park. It's about three hundred miles north of here, in Canada. We'll stay in a campground by the road, but we'll go on some side trips, maybe stay overnight in the wilds."

"Cool!" said Denny with feeling. "I thought we'd be staying someplace around here."

"You'll like it up there. Lots of lakes with big trees around them and loons swimming

in the water and giving out that weird call."
For a moment Rick met Denny's eyes with a
direct, happy look.

"Algonquin's real wild country, isn't it?"
asked Denny.

"Well, it's not all wild. They do some lumbering there. But one place where Dad and
I went we were alone except for the chip-
munks and the bears — and the wolves."

"Wolves? You're kidding."

"Nope. There are a lot of wolves in Algonquin." He looked searchingly at Denny.
"Maybe I'm crazy to take a punk like you
along. You can stay with Aunt Wilma, you
know."

Again Denny was hurt and angry. "No,
thanks," he said abruptly. "Just because I'm
short for my age, you don't have to think I'm
a little kid. How old do you think I am? I'm
thirteen and even if I haven't gone camping
before, I'm not helpless."

"Sorry," said Rick. "I keep forgetting
you're that old. Anyway, you don't have to
worry about seeing any wolves. They stay
away from people." Rick ran his hand
through his dark hair. "Right now I can understand how they feel."

So Rick wanted to be alone, thought Denny.

Had he had a fight with Beth? Was that why he wanted to get away so fast?

Rick stuffed several large plastic garbage bags into a packsack. "We can put our packs into these if it rains. Come on. Let's get the car loaded."

The kitchen door opened directly into the garage. Rick switched on the light and went down the steps with a pack slung over his shoulder.

There were two cars in the large double garage — Vince's station wagon and the secondhand red Volkswagen Rick had gotten in June. He had needed it to get to work. Vince had advanced the money and Rick had made payments to his father all summer. He admitted he had a long way to go before his debt was paid.

"Which car are we going to take?" asked Denny.

"Mine."

"There's more room for all this stuff in the stationwagon. Your father said you could use it."

"I know." Rick dumped a packsack into the trunk of the Volkswagen. "But I'd rather use my own car. Besides, it takes a lot less gas."

"What about the canoe?" Denny glanced at

the rafters above the cars where the dark green aluminum canoe was stored.

"No sweat," said Rick. "I've carried it on the VW before."

They had to open the garage door to get the canoe off the rafters and onto the car. But as soon as it was resting on the racks, Rick again closed the door.

Denny sat down on the steps and watched Rick tie the canoe to the car, fore and aft. He felt tired, more like going to bed than starting on a camping trip. He looked at his watch. Ten after ten.

Just as Rick finished the last knot, the doorbell rang.

Rick stiffened. "Look out the window and see who it is. Don't let them see you."

Denny ran to the living room and came back to report. "Aunt Wilma. We'll have to tell her."

"Oh, no, we won't!"

"If we don't she'll be calling the police to have them track us down."

Rick slapped himself on the forehead. "You're right. But don't tell her where we're going."

"All right." Denny started away. "I'll let her in."

"Let me do the talking," warned Rick.

Secret Journey

Aunt Wilma was a big woman. Rick had once remarked that she reminded him of a lady wrestler.

Denny thought of this as she charged into the living room.

"What took you so long to let me in?" she demanded. "Denny Mitchell, what are you up to? You have a funny look on your face. Where's Rick?"

"Right here, Aunt Wilma," he announced from the kitchen doorway. "Denny and I are getting ready to take a little trip."

"And where, may I ask, are you going?"

"Oh, I can't say exactly. We'll be traveling around."

In the end, Aunt Wilma took the news of their trip better than Denny had expected.

"You're seventeen," she said to Rick. "Old enough to know what you're doing, whether you do or not. And your dad said he'd left you in charge." She looked from one to the other of the boys. "It's a good idea for you to go off together and get to know each other." She heaved herself out of the chair. "Do you have enough money, Rick?"

"Yes," said Rick. "Dad left us enough to last while he and Sara are away, and I have some of my own."

"I have a little, too," volunteered Denny, slapping his hip pocket where he kept his wallet.

Aunt Wilma said, "Call me up every now and then so I know you're still alive. You can call collect."

"OK, Aunt Wilma. We'll keep in touch."

Rick paced to the door and back. Denny could see he was in a hurry to have his aunt leave.

As soon as the door closed behind her, Rick locked it. He whirled around.

"Let's go!"

"You didn't tell her we were leaving to-night."

"She'll find out soon enough. I didn't want to spend any more time talking about it." Rick opened the door to the front closet. "Get yourself a sweater and a heavy jacket. It's cold up there at night. And did you pack an extra pair of shoes?"

"Yes, and my bathing trunks. Hey, Rick, do you have any fish poles?"

"I forgot them! And we'll need them."

Denny said, "While you get them I'm going to call Ted." He had met Ted Quinn only three weeks ago on one of his few trips to the swimming pool in the park, but they had quickly become friends. They saw each other often for he lived only three blocks away.

"No, don't call him." Rick spoke quietly, but his tone was serious. "I'm not even phoning Beth."

Denny could only look at him in amazement. He knew how his stepbrother felt about Beth. He could have a dozen girls if he wanted to, but Beth was the only one he looked at.

"Why not tell Beth and Ted?" asked Denny. "They'll want to know. They'll think we're mad at them." He paused and dared to ask, "Are you mad at Beth?"

Rick took a deep breath as if his chest hurt. "No, I'm not mad at her. But she would ask why we're going and where. And we're not telling anyone where we're going. Or why."

Denny shook his head. He had a helpless feeling. What was wrong with Rick?

"I want to go camping," Denny blurted out, "but I don't like being kept in the dark."

Rick answered with unusual patience. "I don't blame you. I'll clue you in some time. But right now, just take my word for it. It's better not to have anyone know where we're going tonight." He headed for the stairs. "I'll get the fish poles."

Denny sighed. Apparently Rick was through answering questions. Bottling his curiosity, Denny went up to his room. He would get his camera. Might be some swell chances to take pictures. He'd like to snap a photo of a moose or a bear. To do that he should have his telephoto lens. It was heavy to carry, but without it he couldn't get a close view of any animals.

As he opened his desk drawer to get the camera he suddenly remembered that he had promised Ted he'd be at his house tomorrow morning. They planned to take a hike into the woods if the weather was good.

Denny sat down on the chair in front of the desk. Rick was set against his phoning Ted. Besides, at this time of night, Ted might be asleep. How could he let him know the hike was off?

If he wrote a letter, Ted wouldn't get it in time.

Then he thought of the answer. Aunt Wilma. She would be over first thing tomorrow morning to see if they'd gone yet. He'd leave a note for her.

Snatching up a piece of paper, he scrawled:

Dear Aunt Wilma,
    We're going to Algonquin tonight. Will you please phone Ted Quinn and tell him I've gone?

                    Thanks,
                    Denny

Hearing Rick's footsteps on the attic stairs, Denny hastily folded the note and thrust it into his pocket. Probably Rick wouldn't care if he left a note. He just didn't want to answer a lot of questions. Once they were on their way, what difference would it make if Ted and Aunt Wilma knew where they were going?

But no matter what, thought Denny, I have a right to let Ted know I'm going away.

Rick hurried by with the poles in his hand. "Come *on*!" he called.

Denny snatched up the plastic case containing his camera and telephoto lens. Switching off the light, he followed Rick down the stairs.

When Denny reached the first floor, Rick was already getting into the car. Dropping the note on the kitchen table, he ran out to the garage and laid his camera kit on the back seat of the car.

Rick started the VW motor. "Open the garage door," he told Denny. "After I drive out, close it and be sure it's locked and then jump in with me fast."

Denny shut his lips tightly together. More mystery. But he did as his stepbrother asked. He wanted to go on this trip. When they were out of town, he'd try to get Rick to explain.

They started down the driveway. "Hey, your lights aren't on!" Denny said.

"I know it. Don't talk."

The street was quiet. Lights gleamed in most of the houses, but no one was on the sidewalks and they met no cars. Rick left the headlights off until they turned onto a busy cross street.

"Maybe we ought to buy some food," suggested Denny as they passed a supermart that was still open. "There are a lot of things we don't have."

"We'll stock up in Canada," Rick said crisply.

In a few minutes they were on the expressway, headed for Niagara Falls and Canada.

They crossed the Niagara River on the Rainbow Bridge, just below the falls. Looking upstream to his left, Denny could see the colored lights reflected in the spray from the huge cataract.

"It's a good thing you can drive at night," Denny commented. Rick had taken driver education at school, and in June when he had turned seventeen he had gotten a license that gave him the right to drive at night without an adult driver in the car.

The customs officer on the Canadian end of the bridge was friendly.

"Where are you going?" he asked.

"Quebec," said Rick promptly.

Denny stopped himself from protesting that Algonquin wasn't in Quebec. Rick must be trying to cover his trail. Again Denny wondered, why?

The inspector glanced at the canoe. "Kinda late to be starting out on a camping trip, isn't it?"

Rick said easily, "We want to make the most of our free time."

"You bringing that canoe back with you?"

"Oh, yes. We certainly are," said Rick.

"Anything with you besides your personal belongings?"

"No, sir," Rick answered.

"All right. Go ahead. Have a good trip."

They drove up a hill and headed for the Queen Elizabeth Highway.

Rick seemed to relax now that they were across the border. He slapped Denny on the knee. "We're on our way! Great, isn't it?"

Denny's hopes soared at Rick's friendly manner.

The night was warm so they had the windows open. They passed houses where people were sitting on their porches in the dark. Denny caught a faint scent of flowers from the small gardens that bordered most of the lawns.

Soon they left the town and turned right onto the Queen Elizabeth Highway. Here, even at this time of night, the traffic was heavy. It was a four-lane highway with a patch of grass between the east and west roadways. A river of headlights flowed toward them. And in the same lane as the VW were other cars, campers, and huge trucks that rumbled and shook as they went over occasional rough places in the pavement.

The canoe projected over the front and back of the little car like a porch roof, giving Denny a sheltered feeling. He leaned his head against the headrest. Rick was a good driver and he seemed to like driving. Already he had lost his worried look. He had the radio on and was humming along with the tune that was being played.

Denny closed his eyes. This was going to be a swell vacation, after all. Whatever had been bugging Rick, he was OK now. Maybe he was just tired out from working all summer. He'd had a job with a road gang and he had to work hard in the sun and rain, shoveling gravel.

Denny's head dropped to one side. He slid farther down in the seat. He wanted to stay awake to enjoy the trip for he had never before been on this road. But the motion of the car, the music, and the lateness of the hour were overcoming him.

He awakened when the news came on. It was a Buffalo station and the reporter was telling about a power failure in Albany. Then he talked about a bill the President had vetoed and about a prisoner who had escaped from somewhere.

Denny opened his eyes and saw that they were high in the air on a skyway that crossed a bay. On his left lights shone like Christmas decorations on mills and furnaces and large ships that lined the shore of a harbor.

Rick said, "That's Hamilton over there. Big steel-manufacturing city."

When he looked in the opposite direction Denny could see a strip of sand beach and streets of close-ranked cottages. Beyond the beach stretched the blue darkness of Lake Ontario, brightened by a path of moonlight on the waves.

Denny pointed to the circular skeleton of a Ferris wheel. "I sure was crazy about Ferris wheels when I was a kid. Weren't you?"

"Sure, I liked them OK."

"Mom says she never could take me past one. She'd have to stop and let me ride on it."

Rick glanced briefly at Denny. "Sounds like you."

"What do you mean?"

"I bet you always got what you wanted."

"I wouldn't say that," objected Denny.

"I would. I've watched you this past month and I haven't seen you doing anything to help Sara."

"That's not true!"

Rick said, "OK. How many times have you peeled potatoes or cleared up the dishes?"

"That's not my job. Every time I set foot in the kitchen my grandmother used to chase me out."

"Yeah," said Rick thoughtfully, "you and Sara lived with your grandparents after your father died. I suppose they helped to spoil you."

Denny said defensively, "Mom said she didn't know what she'd have done without me."

"Forget I said anything," said Rick. "Sorry I brought it up. Go to sleep."

Denny leaned back and stared out the window. Now he knew why Rick didn't like him. He thought he was a spoiled kid and he didn't do enough to help his mother. Hah! thought Denny. Rick spent enough time in the kitchen for two people. He was always in there when Mom was cooking, and he talked nonstop, until it was a wonder she could cook.

The miles went by in silence except for the drone of the radio. They turned left onto a wide road that led directly north. The traffic thinned out and the few houses and business buildings they passed were dark. The air that came in the windows smelled fresh and cool. Too cool.

Denny rolled up his window and closed his eyes. He didn't see how he could treat his mother any better, and how could he convince Rick he wasn't a spoiled kid?

Tired of his own unhappy thoughts, he fell asleep.

When he awakened they were pulling into a lighted gas station with restaurant attached.

"Hungry?" asked Rick.

Denny sat up straight. "I'll say!"

"This place has pretty good hamburgers. Dad and I had lunch here last summer." Again Rick's tone was friendly. He stopped the car at one of the gas pumps. "Fill it up while we get some food," he told the attendant.

Denny led the way into the restaurant and slid into a booth, taking the seat next to the window and facing the door. He picked up the menu that was propped behind the napkin holder.

Rick hesitated beside the table, looking out the window. Then he said quietly, "Take the other seat, will you? I want to sit there."

Denny said nothing. But as he changed to the other seat an idea clicked into place in his mind. Rick was expecting someone. And he wanted to see them before they saw him. That's why he had asked to change seats, so he could be next to the window and still keep track of the door.

Denny watched his stepbrother over the top of his menu. Sure enough, Rick's eyes darted from the window to the door and back again.

It all tied in with the way he had closed the drapes back home and had been in such a hurry to start on this trip.

Who did he think was coming after him? Whoever it was, Denny was sure Rick was afraid of them.

A Cat and Mouse Game

The waitress set a plate of hamburger and French fries in front of Denny. The rich, warm scent made him realize how hungry he was. He picked up the hamburger and took a large, satisfying bite.

Rick dumped sugar from the container and stirred it into his coffee. The spoon went around and around. Denny raised his eyes to Rick's face. At once he knew by his expression that someone was coming.

Denny twisted around in his seat. The door swung open and the gas station attendant came down the aisle toward them.

"Say, mister," he said to Rick. "Your red Volkswagen out there . . ."

Rick's spoon dropped to the table with a clatter. "Yes, what is it?"

"Your gas tank's leaking."

Rick groaned. "I thought I was using too much gas. How bad is it?"

"Not bad. Just a drip. But it could get worse."

Rick asked hopefully, "Can you fix it?"

"Not me. I'm no mechanic. I just happened to notice this little drip coming out under your car."

"Is there any place around here where I can get it fixed?"

"Nope. The fellow that comes on duty here at eight knows some about cars, but we don't have tools for fixing nothing like a gas leak. You won't find no garage open around here before eight, anyway."

Rick looked at his watch. "It's 3:00 A.M. now. I'm not going to sit around and wait for a garage to open. We'll go on and take our chances."

"Keep an eye on the gauge," advised the attendant. "If it starts going down fast, better put your finger in the hole." He went to the door, grinning to himself.

Rick slid out of his seat and snatched up the check. "Come on. Let's hit the road."

Denny bundled his hamburger and the French fries into his napkin and followed him.

When they came out of the restaurant, Denny was struck by the loneliness of the place. Trees crowded close around the clearing where the gas station stood, and across the road was a dark forest.

What a spot this would be for an ambush! he thought, munching on one of the French fries. A person could drive past in a car, toss out a bomb or a hand grenade, and be gone before anyone would know what had happened.

Denny wiped catsup from his chin and told himself there was no need to get jumpy just because Rick was on edge. People all over the world were throwing bombs at each other, but they had their reasons. Why would anyone bomb Rick and him?

Rick was crouched beside the car staring at the little pool of gasoline under the gas tank. He straightened and glanced around.

"Oh, there you are. Get in." He gave a quick look at the powerful arc lamps that edged the clearing, then hurried to climb into the car as if he couldn't wait to get out of the light.

Denny's curiosity was overcoming his caution. He did not want to rouse Rick's anger, but he had to get some answers.

As soon as they were again on the road, he said, "Rick, what's bothering you?"

"What do you mean?"

"I know something's going on," Denny insisted. "You act like — like — "

Rick grinned unexpectedly. "Like a cat with his tail on fire?"

Denny stared at him, taken by surprise. "Well, yes. What I want to know is, who's chasing you?"

Rick said bluntly, "It's none of your business."

"But it is my business. If you're going to take me up to Algonquin to get away from someone, I have a right to know who we're hiding from." His voice rose. "I want to know — now!"

Rick said, "You sure are persistent. I can see why Sara took you on the Ferris wheel. OK, I'll tell you this much. I'm worried about something, but it doesn't have anything to do with you. Look, I'm taking you on a camping trip and you're going to have a ball."

Denny decided to ignore the crack about the Ferris wheel. "I'm sure glad we're going camping," he said. "But you didn't come up here just to give me a swell time. You came because you're scared of something or somebody back home."

Rick said calmly, "Could be."

"Oh, so you admit it!"

"I don't admit anything. And you might as well stop prying." Rick sounded weary.

Denny glanced at his stepbrother's profile. In the dim light his handsome face looked drawn and worried. Some of Denny's anger melted away. Rick must be in real trouble.

And he brought me along, thought Denny. He must like me a little or he'd have left me home.

Denny cleared his throat and, feeling rather embarrassed, he said, "If I can help, let me know."

Rick said gruffly, "Thanks. I'll keep it in mind."

The little car pushed on through the night.

Denny still didn't know what Rick was running away from but he felt better. He and Rick had taken one step toward each other.

He thought of Aunt Wilma. Would she be upset when she found out they had left on their trip tonight? He hoped she would tell Ted he had gone.

For the first time, Denny began to worry about what Rick would say when he learned about the note on the kitchen table.

Sitting forward, Denny squinted at the gas gauge. Already it was down a little from the full mark. If the leak got worse they might not reach Algonquin Park tonight.

Again Denny slumped down in his seat. He couldn't do anything about the hole in the gas tank and anyway he was too tired to keep his eyes open any longer.

It was an hour later when he was awakened from a sound sleep by the jolting and swaying of the Volkswagen. He sat up and steadied himself by clutching the handle in front of him. Rick had the gas pedal pressed to the floor and he was leaning over the wheel as if he were in the Grand Prix.

"What's the rush?" asked Denny.

Rick kept his eyes on the road. "Someone's following us."

Denny looked back into the glare of headlights set at high beam. He could see nothing but the brilliant lights.

"Maybe it's a police car," he suggested. "You're sure speeding."

Rick said tensely, "They'd have put their flasher on by now. Or a siren."

"Maybe he wants to get past you. Why don't you slow down and give him a chance?"

"Not on your life." Rick didn't slacken his speed. "See if you can make out who's in the car."

Denny looked back. "I can't see a thing. The lights are too bright. Come on. Slow down, Rick. I'm too young to die."

Suddenly Rick obeyed. The needle on the speedometer began to drop. Denny expected the car in the rear to pass them, but it, too, slowed down.

"Now are you satisfied?" Rick asked angrily. "They're playing a cat and mouse game." Again he pressed down the accelerator.

Denny's mouth felt dry. "You think you know who's in that car, don't you?"

Rick did not answer.

Denny unfastened his seatbelt and got onto his knees, looking over the back of the seat at the pursuing car.

"Keep down!" snapped Rick. "Do you want to get your head blown off?"

Denny dropped down in his seat and faced the front. "You told me to look a minute ago!"

"Sorry. Now I'm *sure* who it is."

Denny crouched lower. The back of his neck felt cold as if the muzzle of a gun were pressed against it.

"Do you think they're going — to shoot through the window?" he asked.

"Who knows?"

The inside of the Volkswagen began to get brighter. Denny did not turn around, but he knew without looking that the car behind them was pulling closer.

"Now what's he up to?" muttered Rick.

Ahead of them was the white framework of a bridge. The roadway across it was only two lanes wide.

As the VW approached the bridge, the other car, a yellow, four-door Chevrolet, moved to the left as if about to pass them.

Good riddance! thought Denny. They were stupid to pass on a narrow bridge, but at least there was nothing coming from the other direction.

But instead of passing, the yellow Chevy

crowded closer to the VW, forcing it to the right.

Denny stared in horror as they headed directly for the white metal framework of the bridge truss. Rick had slowed down, and now he jammed on the brakes, but it seemed impossible that he could stop in time. Denny braced himself for the crash.

Narrow Escape

The crash did not come. Rick pulled hard to the right onto the shoulder of the road. For a sickening moment it seemed certain that they would tip over. In spite of his seatbelt, Denny was flung to the side and then forward and back as the VW, still rocking, came to a screeching halt at a right angle to the road.

The driver's side of the car was only inches from the bridge truss.

The car that had been following them went on across the bridge and continued up the road, weaving crazily back and forth. A man in the back seat thrust his head out the window and waved at them.

"The fools!" exclaimed Rick.

Denny was unhurt but breathless after the narrow escape. "We're lucky we aren't wrapped around this bridge!"

"We would be if I hadn't slowed down when they started to pass. Did you get a look at them?"

"It was too dark," said Denny. "It was a Canadian license plate, though. I saw that when our headlights hit it. And I think there were several people in the car."

Rick's hands were shaking but Denny thought he acted less worried. "Looked to me like a car full of drunks," he said. "Probably been out celebrating all night. I'm going to report them when we get to the next police station. They could kill somebody — or themselves."

"Do you think one of them is the guy who's after you?"

"I don't believe so. I think he'd be alone."

Rick fell silent, then he added, "Of course he might have someone with him."

Rick tried to open his door but it was too close to the bridge truss. "It's your move!" he said to Denny.

The boys climbed out and examined the VW. The canoe had slipped to one side, so they unfastened it and set it onto the roadside grass. Then, with Denny directing him, Rick backed the car away from the bridge and parked it on the shoulder of the road.

There seemed to be no damage to the VW. After returning the canoe to the top of the car, they again headed north.

A few miles farther on they passed a police car at the side of the road with its red bubble flashing. In front of it was the yellow Chevrolet. A policeman was talking to the driver and writing out a summons.

"Good," remarked Rick. "We don't have to stop at the police station. By the way, I got a good look at the men in that car and I don't know any of them." He said apologetically, "I don't know why I was so sure that car was following me. No one knows where I am — not even Beth or Aunt Wilma. But doggone it, I still have the feeling I'm not safe."

Denny twisted uneasily in his seat. Right

now he should confess that soon Aunt Wilma would have that information. But knowing how furious Rick would be, he couldn't get up the courage to speak about the note.

I didn't have to mention to Aunt Wilma that we were going to Algonquin, he admitted to himself. All I had to say was we were leaving on a trip. Period.

Half an hour later, they rolled down the main street of the town of Huntsville. At the foot of the hill on his left, Denny could see a river with piles of lumber stacked on its banks.

"That's the Muskoka River," Rick said. "I suppose it's one reason the town started here. The railroad's another reason. But I know they used the water for power to run the sawmill. Lumbering is still big up here. The biggest business now is taking care of tourists, though."

In less than an hour they came to a halt beside a narrow stone gatehouse that sat between the east and west lanes of the road.

Rick paid the admission fee and then drove between the gateposts under the nose of a large carved bear. They were inside Algonquin Park at last.

The trees had been cut back on either side

of the road as if there were danger that the forest would swallow the pavement if given a chance. The flowers and weeds that grew in this grassy strip were pale gold in the path of the headlights. Now and then a break in the solid bank of trees showed the gleam of a lake.

"Watch for a campground," said Rick. "With this leaky tank I want to stop in the first place we find."

But they were twenty miles into the park before they found a campground that was not full.

"Mew Lake," said Rick. "Say, this is where Dad and I stayed."

"I thought you took a canoe trip."

Rick said irritably, "We did. But first we camped a few days at Mew Lake. I like this place and I know my way around it."

The campground was quiet and dark. No one was in the small office beside the entrance.

"So we don't have to register tonight." Rick sounded pleased.

"We don't have to pay then?"

"Oh, sure. Tomorrow we'll pay and I'll have to sign my name and address on the dotted line. But right now no one in the world knows we're here. For what's left of tonight we're as safe as fleas on a lame dog."

"You still think someone's chasing you?" asked Denny as they drove down the sandy road.

This time Rick surprised him by admitting, "I have it on good authority that someone's looking for me — a man named Leach. And he isn't the type who gives up easy. He might even have been watching the house when we left tonight."

"Why is this guy Leach looking for you?"

Rick kept turning his head to the right and then to the left, searching for an empty campsite. "Stow it, Denny. How can I find a campsite with you yammering at me? And you might help me look, y'know."

I wasn't yammering, thought Denny. He wondered why he always rubbed Rick the wrong way.

They drove up and down roads that wound through the campground. Each campsite had its own fireplace and table and a flat space for a tent or trailer or camper, but as far as Denny could see, every site was full.

They reached a road that ran beside Mew Lake. The moon, almost full, was sinking behind the hill on the far side of the lake. Its last rays gave the water a silvery look.

Rick turned left and drove on slowly. Again every spot was occupied until, almost at the end of the road, just past a large trailer, Denny saw an empty campsite beside the water.

"There's a place!" he exclaimed.

"Couldn't be better," said Rick in a satisfied tone. "We're as far from the highway as we can get."

Denny tried to help put up the tent, but after one end collapsed on his head and the tent stakes he put in pulled out of the ground, Rick said, "I'll finish this. You get out the sleeping bags and lock up the car."

What a dope I am! thought Denny.

When he had locked the car, he watched Rick, admiring the efficient way he worked. In less than ten minutes, the tent was up.

It was a small tent, just high enough in the center for Rick to sit up. Not even Denny could stand upright in it. Still, it was a good tent in many ways, Denny thought. He liked the way the floor was attached to the sides and the way the mosquito netting could be zipped shut. As a protection against bears, the tent was worthless, but at least it would keep out bugs.

Rick tossed the sleeping bags into the tent.

"I don't care what you do. I'm beat," he said. "I'm crawling in the sack."

Denny looked around. No canoes or boats were in sight on the lake. Not far out on the water two large birds that looked like ducks were swimming. Those must be the loons Rick had mentioned.

Their campsite was sheltered by a row of spruce trees, but between the branches Denny could see another tent not far away, and the large trailer that they had passed on the way in. There was no sign of life in either one.

"I might as well sleep, too," he said. He followed Rick into the tent and zipped the mosquito netting shut.

As he lay in his sleeping bag, his last waking thoughts were of the mysterious person who had frightened Rick into taking this trip. At least he had a name — Leach. What did he look like? And what had Rick done to make him an enemy?

A Day with Holly

Rick got up at eight o'clock.

"Can you fix yourself some breakfast?" he asked Denny who was pulling on a sweater against the morning chill.

"Sure." Denny was not going to admit to Rick that he rarely fixed his own breakfast and that he didn't have much of an idea how to cook over a campfire.

Rick unlocked the VW. "I want to get this

car to a garage. Probably a lot of cars ahead of me already," he said gloomily. "I could be gone all day. Depends on how soon they can fix this gas tank."

"Just one thing," said Denny. "What does this guy Leach look like? He might come nosing around here when you're gone."

Rick paused with his hand on the door handle. "You're safe enough. He wouldn't know you from Adam."

"Just the same, I ought to know how he looks," argued Denny. "Then I can tell you if he's been around."

"Think of an ape," said Rick. "An ape with a lot of curly brown hair."

"Ugly-looking face?"

"No. Not bad looking, except when he's mad. Then he can look mean enough." Rick pulled open the door. "I have to be on my way."

Denny stopped him again. "Wait! Don't go off with my camera." He reached into the car and took his camera kit from the back seat. "I may take some pictures today."

As Rick started the car, he said warningly, "If you build a fire, be sure you put it out."

"Natch," said Denny. He wondered why he had ever thought he wanted a brother, especially this one who didn't think he even knew enough to put out a campfire.

Yet when Rick drove off, he felt deserted. What could he do all alone in a strange campground? And come to think of it, he was hungry.

In the food bag he found bread, oleo, and cheese from which he made himself a sandwich. There was bacon but that would take too long to cook. Maybe he'd try making a fire at lunch time if Rick was still gone.

The sun had risen high enough to warm the clearing where the tent stood and Denny began to feel more cheerful.

He was heading toward the main road of the camp on a search for drinking water when he passed the trailer he had noticed the night before. A girl about his own age was standing beside it. She was dressed in blue shorts and shirt and she wore her straight blond hair in a pixie cut.

"Hi!" she greeted him. "Looking for something?"

Denny stopped. "Hi. Yeah. Is there any drinking water around here?"

"Yes." The girl pointed. "You go down that way to the first road. Then you turn right, then left."

"I'm lost already," complained Denny.

The girl laughed. "Come on. I'll show you."

As he walked down the road with the girl beside him, Denny felt happier. Being alone, even in a beautiful camp beside a lake, wasn't much fun. He noted with satisfaction that the girl was no taller than he.

"I'm Holly Adams," she said. "We live down near Toronto and we've been here three days."

"Denny Mitchell from Buffalo, New York."

"You must have come last night," said Holly. "You weren't here when I went to bed."

Denny liked the look of this girl. He liked the way she showed her square white teeth when she smiled and he liked the direct gaze of her blue eyes.

When they returned with Denny's plastic jug full of water, Holly asked, "Have you been swimming yet?"

"No."

"Want to go?"

"I sure do."

"We'll have to take my little brother Oliver. I have to help take care of him."

Denny was sorry to hear that. A little kid could be a real pain to have around. He supposed they'd have to stay in the shallow water with him all the time. Probably he'd yell a lot.

But Oliver turned out to be a sturdy little

four-year-old who took an instant liking to Denny. He had no fear of the water and already he could do a dog paddle. Denny began to teach him to lie on his face in the water and kick his feet.

"He'll soon be doing the crawl," he told Holly.

The friendliness of this brother and sister was a comfort after Rick's criticism.

When they were tired of the water, Denny and Holly helped Oliver build a garage in the sand for his toy trucks.

"You have a way with kids," remarked Holly.

"I always wanted a brother."

"But you have one!" said Holly in surprise.

"Rick's my stepbrother, and he's only been that for a month." He bent his head over the sand garage. "One month too long."

For a moment Holly said nothing; then she asked quietly, "He isn't what you expected?"

"He's so — critical!" Denny burst out.

"About what?"

Denny's face reddened. "He thinks I don't help my mother enough."

Holly said calmly, "Do you?"

"I thought I did. But now when I look back, I don't know." He sighed. "I shouldn't tell you my problems."

49

"Yes, you should. You have to talk to someone."

He was too embarrassed to look at her, but he managed to say, "It helps, I guess."

"Is that your only problem?"

"No. Rick says I'm clumsy about doing things like putting up the tent." Denny frowned. "What does he expect?"

Holly said matter-of-factly, "You can learn."

"Yeah, I suppose so. But not with Rick around. When he's watching me, I'm all thumbs."

Holly's eyes rested thoughtfully on Oliver. "Even if Rick was your own brother, you might not like him all the time. My girl friend back home has a brother and they fight with each other a lot. But he won't let anyone else pick on her. When she needs him, he's there."

They sat for a while in silence. Then Holly looked up at the sky. "Must be about lunch time."

"Yeah. Guess I'd better start practicing my fire building."

"Later," said Holly. "Right now you're going to have lunch with us. Mom told me to ask you."

"Great!"

"Oh, I'd better warn you about Dad."

Denny grinned. "Is he dangerous?"

"Oh, you! Of course not. But he's hipped on ecology. He talks about air pollution and saving the wild lands and stuff like that all the time. Be prepared for a big lecture."

"I'll bet he can't tell me anything I haven't heard already."

They ate at the picnic table outside the trailer. Mrs. Adams, a small blond woman with a warm smile, brought out homemade chicken soup and corn muffins she had baked in the tiny kitchen of the trailer.

"Holly tells me you and your brother are going to take some canoe trips on the lakes," said Mr. Adams. He, too, was blond, though Denny noticed he was getting bald on top.

"Yes, sir," said Denny.

"That's just great. As soon as Oliver's old enough we'd like to take trips like that. This is a good time to go. The black flies are gone in August." Mr. Adams looked at Denny thoughtfully. "Got your supplies, I suppose?"

"Not everything. Rick — that's my step-brother — is going to buy some more food today."

Mr. Adams said, "I hope he knows he's not supposed to take cans and bottles into the interior unless he's going to bring them out again. By the way, are you and your brother interested in ecology?"

Denny wanted to be honest. "Well, sort of."

"You should be," said Mr. Adams severely. "We'd all better be interested in taking care of the earth. At the rate we're going we'll soon have it worn out. We're messing up the balance of nature, too. Take the wolf, for instance."

Denny almost choked on his soup. What did the wolf have to do with ecology? Holly was smiling at him with a What-did-I-tell-you look.

Mr. Adams asked, "What do you know about wolves, Denny?"

"Well, they're wild animals and they howl and they're dangerous. They eat deer and maybe people, and I hope we don't meet any of them while we're camping."

"You see?" Mr. Adams looked at his wife and Holly. "We have to educate this boy."

Mrs. Adams said in her gentle way, "You don't have to be afraid of wolves, Denny. There are many packs of timber wolves in this park, but no person has ever been attacked by a wolf in Algonquin."

"That's right," agreed Mr. Adams. "And as to the deer, of course the wolves kill some healthy ones, but it's easier for them to catch the weakest. That leaves mainly the strong ones to breed. Strange as it sounds, the wolves are good for the deer."

"Let's take him on the wolf howl tonight!" suggested Holly.

Mr. Adams said, "Sure. Glad to have him. And this afternoon how about a hike on the Beaver Pond Trail? We can show Denny how the beaver made a pond where there wasn't any pond before."

By the time Rick came back with the Volkswagen late that afternoon, Denny had taken a roll of pictures of beaver dams and Holly and lakes surrounded by white birch trees. He was a convert to the idea of keeping nature in balance and he felt as if he had known the Adams family for years.

To Denny's surprise, his stepbrother said nothing about the man named Leach. In fact, he seemed quite relaxed.

"The car's fixed," he said, "but it took a lot of our cash, and the groceries cost plenty, too. I found a store up the road that specializes in freeze-dried foods, but it's expensive stuff. They've got everything — scrambled eggs, dried fruit, cocoa mix. You name it and if you can pay for it you can have it.

Denny asked anxiously, "You didn't get any canned food, did you?"

"No. Why?"

"Cans aren't good for the environment."

Rick gave Denny a puzzled look, but he said only, "Oh, I know that. Incidentally, I bought a fishing license. We can catch some of our own food."

"I want to fish, too," said Denny. "Did you get a license for me?"

"I got one that covers both of us. By the way, what'll we have for supper?"

"Forget it," said Denny. "We're invited out for dinner. I met the people in that trailer over there. Their name is Adams and they're great."

Rick raised his eyebrows. "You're a fast worker. I have to hand it to you, Denny. People like you."

"Thanks."

"It's the truth. I hope you didn't tie us up for the whole evening, though. I only got a couple of hours sleep last night and I want to hit the sack early."

"You can sleep if you want to. But I'm going on a wolf howl."

"A what?"

"Never mind," said Denny. "I'll tell you all about it when I come back." Let him wonder for a while and see how he likes it, thought Denny.

The Wolf Howl

Rick was already asleep in the tent when Mr. Adams, Holly, and Denny left for the wolf howl.

"The program starts at nine," Mr. Adams said as they drove out of the Mew Lake Campground, "but we want to be there early to get a good seat."

The wolf howl was still a mystery to Denny. "What's it all about?" he asked. He was in the front seat with Holly and her father.

Mr. Adams said, "The park naturalists — they're like your forest rangers in the States — will howl at the wolves and try to get the wolves to howl back. But first we're going to the Pog Lake Amphitheater to see a movie on wolves and get briefed on wolf howling."

"It's great!" Holly assured Denny. "We went on two wolf howls last year. One time we heard the wolves and the other time we didn't. Here's hoping they howl tonight."

Mr. Adams turned east onto the main road. The traffic was heavy and most of it seemed to be going with them.

At the Pog Lake lot, several naturalists were directing the traffic.

When they had parked, Mr. Adams, Holly, and Denny followed the crowds down a dimly lighted path. People were talking in quiet voices but Denny sensed an air of unusual excitement.

The amphitheater was a large clearing with logs split lengthways through the center for seats. Denny and his new friends found places halfway to the front and sat down to wait. The stage which they faced was dark and empty but a few lights shone on posts around the edge of the clearing.

As Denny's eyes became more accustomed to the semi-darkness, he watched the people who came down the aisles searching for seats.

He began to study their faces and suddenly he wondered if one of these people might be Leach, the man of whom his stepbrother was afraid. This would be the kind of place where he might expect to find Rick.

I wonder if Leach has found out what I look like? thought Denny.

He wondered, too, what Leach would do to Rick if he found him. What if Leach came to the Mew Lake Campground this evening? He might look at the papers on which campers registered.

Denny pictured his stepbrother lying asleep in the tent and could imagine Leach, a shadowy figure, creeping up on him. There beside the lake Rick was quite alone, for most of the campers had come on the wolf howl.

Of course Mrs. Adams was nearby. She had stayed at the trailer with Oliver because she hadn't wanted to keep the little fellow up so late.

"You won't be home until midnight," she

had said. "And I've been on wolf howls before. I have a good book to read and I'll be happy."

So Rick wasn't completely alone, but what could Mrs. Adams do if Leach came after him? For a moment Denny wondered if he should ask Mr. Adams to take him back to camp.

Then he thought reasonably, Rick wouldn't have stayed at Mew Lake if he hadn't felt safe. He hadn't said anything about Leach today. Maybe he had gotten over being scared.

"Denny!" Holly pulled at his sleeve.

Denny turned, slowly coming back to the present. "What?"

"What's the matter?" Holly asked. "I've been trying to talk to you and you didn't act like you heard me."

"Sorry. I was thinking about something else." He wished he could tell her about Rick's fear of Leach, but he was sure his stepbrother wouldn't like him to say anything. It was Rick's problem and Denny felt he didn't have any right to talk about it. It was bad enough that he had already complained to her about Rick's critical attitude.

Holly pointed to the stage. "Look, the lights are coming on."

Denny was glad they had arrived early because now every seat was taken and lines of people stood all around the edge of the open-air theater.

One of the park naturalists walked onto the stage, carrying a microphone.

"My name is Sam Kosac," he said. "Welcome to the third wolf howl of the season. All the conditions are right for us tonight. It's clear and there's no wind. We located a wolf pack last night, so with luck we should be able to hear their voices."

Denny forgot his worries about Leach as Mr. Kosac told how the wolf howl program had started when someone had discovered that captive wolves would answer when a person howled at them.

"A few years ago we were trying to find out how many wolf packs there were in the park and where they were staying," explained the naturalist. "And we were having trouble. Wolves are shy and it was hard to find them, even by airplane. Then we discovered that we could go out at night and imitate their howl and sometimes get an answer. Before long we had most of the packs located. We enjoyed hearing them howl so much we decided to share the fun with you."

By now it was dark enough to show the movie on wolves, and after that Mr. Kosac explained how the cars would follow in line down the road on the way to the spot where the naturalists would howl and try to contact the wolves.

"If the wolves don't answer our first howl, we'll keep trying for a while," said Mr. Kosac. "But once they answer, that's it for the night. We've discovered it takes them half an hour or so to make up their minds to howl again."

As soon as Mr. Kosac left the stage, people rushed from the amphitheater.

More than half the cars were out of the parking lot when the Adams car joined the line that wound its way to the main road and then turned to the west. As they went over a low hill, Denny could see the tail lights a mile ahead and, looking back, headlights far behind.

It was almost an hour later by the time the cars were parked on both sides of the road. Mr. Kosac and two other naturalists walked down the line and stopped near the Adams car which was near the center.

Although there were hundreds of people standing in the dark, there was not a sound.

No car doors slammed and even the little children were quiet.

In the silence, Denny could hear the naturalists talking over their walkie-talkies to their fellow workers at either end of the long lines of cars. The men waited until there was no traffic on the road. Then Mr. Kosac lifted his head and howled.

The sound was so wolflike that Denny looked sharply at the naturalist to be sure it came from his throat. The howl did not last long. Then the men waited and so did the hundreds of people beside the road. But no answer came from the low, level land which they faced.

Mr. Kosac shifted his position and whispered to his companions. Denny was disappointed. Was tonight to be one of the times when the wolves didn't answer?

Now the three naturalists howled together. It must be what the speaker tonight had called a "group howl," Denny decided.

The silence that followed the group howl was complete. How strange, thought Denny. All of these people and no one says a word. The full moon, high in the east, whitened the ground. It was so bright it made the stars seem pale.

Denny had just located the big dipper when a sound came from someplace far out on the level land. It was a mysterious sound, the howl of wolves.

Denny looked toward Holly, and he knew at once by her shining eyes that she had heard the wolves and was as excited as he.

It wasn't a frightening sound, not to people who knew something about wolves. It was almost like music. And to think that they were answering the howl of the men! Denny wondered if he could get wolves to answer him. Mr. Kosac had suggested that sometime they should try do-it-yourself howling.

Too soon the howling stopped. There was a sigh as people shuffled their feet and returned to the world of humans and climbed back into their cars.

On the way back down the road, Denny, Holly, and her father had little to say. They were still under the spell of the voices from the wilderness.

How many girls, or boys, either, would know enough to keep still? thought Denny. He was glad he had been with Holly when he heard the wolves howl. It made another tie between them.

Flight from Mew Lake

A few campfires still burned as Mr. Adams drove through the Mew Lake Campground. Now and then Denny saw a tent that glowed from a light inside. They passed a trailer where two men and two women sat at a table playing cards. But for the most part, the campers seemed to be asleep. People went to bed early when they didn't have electric lights or TV.

Mr. Adams pulled into the space beside the trailer.

Denny jumped out of the car. "Thanks, Mr. Adams. I sure enjoyed it."

"Wait a minute, Denny. I'll walk you home."

"You don't have to. I have a flashlight." Denny didn't want to be a bother. Besides, he felt like being alone and thinking about the sound of the wolves and the whole happy evening.

Holly got out of the car and stood beside him. " 'Bye, Denny. It was fun, wasn't it?"

"The greatest." He wanted to say something more so she'd know what this day had meant to him, but he couldn't find words. "See you tomorrow."

He walked quickly down the sandy road with its smooth mat of pine needles. After he had gone a few yards he turned around. Holly was still standing beside the car and he waved to her. She waved back.

What a swell girl. He had never met another like her. For Pete's sake! he thought. I suppose that's the way old Rick feels about Beth.

He walked easily down the road. The moon gave so much light he turned off his flashlight. Just ahead was the row of spruce trees that shielded his campsite. Denny wondered if Rick were still asleep.

He passed the spruces and stopped in amazement. Their tent was gone! His first thought was — Leach came and took Rick away! His eyes darted across the campsite to the Volkswagen. At least that was still there. And the canoe was again on top of it.

Then he saw Rick. He was coming up from the beach, walking quickly.

"I thought you'd never get here!" he exclaimed. "Get in the car and don't waste time asking questions." He sounded furious.

Denny ignored the request. "Where's the tent?"

"Packed," said Rick. "Everything's in the car. We're leaving."

"Now?"

"Now." Rick slid into the driver's seat and turned on the ignition.

Denny got in beside him, beginning to boil. He was tired of being ordered around without any explanation and he was disheartened by the cold fury in Rick's voice. What have I done *now*? he wondered.

Rick pulled quickly onto the road.

"Let me out at the trailer," said Denny. "I want to tell Holly we're going."

"We don't have time." Rick did not slacken his speed.

"I don't even have her address!" cried Denny. "And she doesn't know how to get in touch with me, either!"

"Sorry," said Rick, but he did not sound sorry. "You're lucky I waited for you."

"I'm not so sure I'm lucky," said Denny bitterly.

They reached the main road and, to Denny's surprise, Rick turned right, heading east.

"Where are we going?" he asked.

"South. To a place where Dad and I went."

"South?" asked Denny, puzzled. "I thought this road went east and west across the park. I didn't see a road on the map going south."

"We're going by canoe." Rick's voice was still tight with anger.

"We're going canoeing *now*? In the middle of the night?"

"There's moonlight. It'll be like day on the water."

Denny said stubbornly, "I'm not going. Not till you tell me what this is all about. I don't see why we couldn't stay at Mew Lake to-night."

"Because I have a selfish desire to stay alive!" Rick burst out.

"Aw, come off it, Rick. Leach won't ever find you up here."

"That's where you're wrong. Thanks to you, he knows exactly where to find me."

Denny felt as if he had been hit in the stomach. "What do you mean?"

"I mean," said Rick slowly, deliberately, "you left a note at the house." Suddenly he struck the instrument panel with his fist. "Dammit! Why did you do it? You knew I didn't want anyone to find out where we were going!"

Denny wanted to shrink through the floor of the car. "I left a note for Aunt Wilma so she'd tell Ted I couldn't come to his house to-day. I didn't see what harm that could do. How'd you find out about it?"

"From Aunt Wilma. I called her tonight after you left on that wolf howl."

"I still don't see — " puzzled Denny. "Aunt Wilma didn't tell Leach, did she?"

"She didn't have to. Where did you leave that note?" demanded Rick.

"On the kitchen table."

"Well, do you know where Aunt Wilma found it? On the floor, crumpled in a ball." Rick grasped the wheel tightly in both hands. "Leach broke into our house last night and read that note and tossed it on the floor!"

"How do you know it was Leach? Did they catch him?"

"No, they didn't catch him, worse luck. But who else would break in and not take a thing? I knew he'd come after me. That's why I left town."

Denny began to understand. "That phone call the night we left. I thought it was Beth, but you didn't talk long enough. Was that Leach?"

"No. That was a friend of mine, warning me that Leach was looking for me with murder in mind. I was sure I'd be safe up here. And I would have been if you hadn't made it good and clear where he could find me. What a sneaky brat you turned out to be!"

Denny tried to explain. "I didn't mean to get you in trouble. If you'd told me before we started that you were in danger I wouldn't have left that note."

"I *told* you I didn't want anyone to know where we were! That should've been enough." Rick glanced nervously at a passing car.

Denny searched for a ray of hope. "You're not sure it was Leach who broke in. And anyway I didn't mention your name in my note."

"It was Leach, all right, and he'll be able to figure it out that I went with you. And even if he couldn't, Aunt Wilma made it clear to the police."

"Oh, she told the police where we'd gone?"

"Naturally. She found the back door had been forced open so she reported it. Of course the police wanted to know where the family was and she told them Dad and Sara were in Bermuda and you and I were in Algonquin. She even told them we had taken the canoe and the camping gear."

"Good night!" exclaimed Denny. "How'd she know that?"

"How do you suppose? She went through the house and attic and garage. Good old nosy Aunt Wilma!"

"She oughta be a detective," commented Denny.

Rick mused unhappily, "It'll probably all be in the newspaper. Maybe it's been on radio and TV already. I don't know if we're safe anyplace in the park, now. I thought we'd stay at Mew Lake and take canoe trips out from there. Now we're stuck. We have to go to the back country where Leach can't get to us so easy."

"I don't see why you didn't call the police back home as soon as you heard this character was out to kill you," said Denny. "You could've asked them to put a guard around the house."

"I should've called them," Rick admitted. "I guess I panicked. All I could think of was getting far away. Anyway," he added, "what good would it do? If all the police and secret service men couldn't keep Jack and Bobby Kennedy and Martin Luther King from getting shot, what chance do I have?"

"I suppose you're right," admitted Denny.

Rick said with feeling, "You know it! And I couldn't leave you home alone in case Leach came along and decided to take his grudge out on you."

So Rick hadn't brought him because he wanted his company, after all. "I don't know why you bothered," Denny said.

"I bothered," said Rick, "because I couldn't face Sara if anything happened to you."

"You're crazy about my mother, aren't you?" Denny lashed out, wanting to hurt his stepbrother. "Maybe you're the one who should've married her instead of your father."

Rick's voice shook. "I'm not crazy about Sara. I love her. I know a wonderful woman when I see one. She's the best thing that ever happened to my father — and me."

"I'm sorry," Denny apologized. "I shouldn't have said what I did. I was just mad."

Rick drew a deep breath. "I know it, Denny. We're not accomplishing anything by all this fighting. If we're going to get out of this alive, we have to pull together. But don't you spring any more suprises like that note! Right?"

"Right. But Rick, I think you ought to go on to the police."

"How's that?"

"The Canadian police. You know, I've seen their cars. Says OPP on the door."

"Ontario Provincial Police," Rick explained absentmindedly. "Yeah. I suppose we could tell them to be on the lookout for Leach. If we pass a phone booth I'll make a call."

But five minutes later Rick jammed on the brakes. "That's the place. I remember those big rocks, and then the bog." He looked back. "The coast is clear. I'll turn around."

Rick did a rapid U-turn and pulled onto the shoulder.

Denny looked around. On both sides of the

road the flat swampy land that Rick called a bog glistened in the moonlight. Directly ahead of the car was a guard rail above a stream that flowed under the road.

"Aren't you going to call the police before we head for the back country?" asked Denny.

"It's more important for me to get out of sight," Rick said. "The Ontario police may be looking for Leach, anyway. I think the police back home would've sent them his description on the chance that he might skip the country."

Denny was bewildered. "Why are the police looking for Leach? Do they know he broke into the house? Or that he's after you?"

"No, no!" Rick sounded impatient. "They've got their own reasons for looking for him. He's an escaped convict. He got away a couple of days ago when he was being taken from one jail to another. He was in for a long term — for murder."

The Choked Stream

Denny cried, "Murder! You're kidding!"

"No way!" Rick seemed amused at Denny's reaction. "I told you he wanted to kill me. You might know he's for real."

"I thought you were putting me on. How did you get mixed up with a murderer?"

"It's a long story. I may tell you some time.

And maybe not." Rick pulled the key out of the ignition. "But definitely not now."

He got out of the car and scanned the road. When he discovered it was deserted in both directions he seemed satisfied.

"We'll put the canoe in the water here and load our packs in it," he said.

Denny looked down the steep slope to the water. Tall weeds grew on the bank and in the drainage ditch at the bottom. Just above the stream was a jumble of boulders.

"Looks like rough going," he said.

"Dad and I made it, so you can. It hasn't changed since we were here. I'll take the canoe and you bring the packs."

Denny remembered all too well Rick's remarks about his being a spoiled kid, so he helped untie the canoe and steadied it while Rick hoisted it onto his shoulders. He was determined not to give his stepbrother another chance to say he didn't do his share of the work. He was already in enough trouble with Rick over the note he had left for Aunt Wilma.

Pulling out one of the packs, Denny slid his arms into the straps and picked his way down the steep bank, skirting the pile of boulders.

At the bottom of the slope he felt cold water from the drainage ditch soaking through the canvas of his sneakers, but he said nothing. No complaining, he reminded himself.

Ahead of him Rick was clambering over the rocks. With one sure movement he flipped the canoe into the water with a gentle splash.

He sure is strong! thought Denny. He wondered if he'd ever be as tall and muscular as his stepbrother.

Leaving the packsack on the boulders, he went back up the slope for the second one.

Rick caught up with him at the car. "You can carry this bag of food along with the other pack, can't you?" he asked.

"Sure!" replied Denny. I will, he thought, if I break my back. "By the way, where's my camera?"

"In the pack with our clothes." Rick closed the trunk of the VW. "Put the stuff in the canoe and wait for me there. I'm going to run the car up the road to a parking lot about a quarter of a mile from here, maybe less. "See you in a few minutes." He paused before starting away. "There's a flashlight in the pocket of that pack, and the life jackets are inside it. Get them out, will you?"

In spite of the moon, it was dark at the foot of the bank. Denny was glad to have the flashlight. He fished out the life jackets and put one on. It was large even worn over his windbreaker.

The canoe, tied to a bush, was floating close to shore, almost hidden by the tall reeds that choked the stream. Standing knee-deep in the chilly water, Denny untied the paddles that were still fastened to the thwarts. When he had the packs and food bag settled in the bottom of the canoe, he used the rope to tie the cargo in place.

If the canoe tipped over, he reasoned, at least they wouldn't lose all their equipment. He thought of the plastic bags Rick had packed. Maybe he should put the packs in those bags, but he was discouraged at the idea of looking for them in the dark.

Denny turned off the flashlight and sat down on a rock to wait for his stepbrother. Here by the stream the air was cool and damp. He zipped up his jacket beneath the life preserver and tried to forget his cold, wet feet.

Once in a while a car sped by on the road overhead. The people who traveled past would never guess there was anyone sitting in the shadows below the road, thought Denny.

Something splashed in the culvert that carried the stream under the road. Denny leaned forward to peer into the huge metal pipe. He could look clear through it to the dim light on the far side of the road, but he couldn't see what had made the splash. He had never before seen such a large culvert. He guessed that it must be fifteen feet in diameter.

A frog leaped into the water beside the canoe, and the sound so close to him made Denny jump. He wished Rick would hurry. It was spooky sitting here alone.

He began to wonder about the man who was chasing his stepbrother. Maybe Leach had arrived in Algonquin by now and was cruising down this road. What if he saw Rick go into the parking lot and went in after him? Denny shivered. Why did Leach want to kill Rick? That was the next thing he had to find out.

His eyes were becoming accustomed to the dim light and he noticed a narrow footbridge about ten feet to his right spanning the stream. There was a path up there, too, leading to the footbridge. At the far end of it he could see two huge rocks that stood on either side of the path like sentinels. Even as he stared, he saw a tall, dim figure leave the shadow between the large rocks and come toward him on the path.

Denny sat motionless, watching. Who would be walking down that path this time of night? He could think only of the killer. He had found Rick and now he was coming to finish off Rick's companion.

It was a frightening thought, but Denny was not actually afraid. He felt as if he were watching a detective story on TV. It wasn't real, and it was bound to come out all right in the end.

The dim figure became a man, and Denny recognized Rick's athletic stride. He was moving quickly and soon his steps sounded on the wooden footbridge. Seconds later, he slid down the grassy bank and joined Denny.

"Hop in!" he said breathlessly. "I hope you can paddle."

"Well, no," Denny admitted. "But it shouldn't be too hard to learn."

Rick groaned. "Get in the bow. The front seat."

"I know the bow from the stern," said Denny irritably.

"Don't be touchy. Remember our new policy — togetherness. The two musketeers." Rick untied the rope from the bush and they drifted into the stream while he fastened his life preserver. "We're going under the road," he said.

It was dark in the culvert and when Denny

accidentally touched the aluminum canoe with his paddle, the sound echoed loudly. In here the water was open with none of the reeds that he had noticed before. Why was that? Then he thought of the answer. There was no sunlight under the culvert so plants didn't grow.

Sure enough, as they came out on the far side of the road, the water was again cluttered with reeds.

Rick spoke up. "Don't try to steer. I'll take care of that. And don't dip your paddle too deep or you'll break it on the bottom. It's shallow here."

"Yeah?" Denny had his doubts. "I had the paddle in deep already and I didn't hit bottom." To prove his point he thrust the paddle straight down into the dark water. Down, down it went.

"Good night!" he exclaimed. "There's no bottom!" He pulled on the paddle and it came out slowly with a sucking noise, dripping with black mire. "Ugh! I wouldn't want to fall into this stuff! Must be quicksand."

Rick said, "Cool it! That isn't quicksand. It's just silt that's collected on the bottom of the stream."

At first the canoe moved easily, for a narrow path of open water ran between the reeds.

On either side of the stream the land was level and swampy and covered with long marsh grass. Here and there the stalks of dead trees gave the bog the look of an old battlefield.

Eager to prove his ability, Denny put all of his strength into every stroke. Soon he had to rest his aching arms.

"Easy does it," said Rick. "A slow, steady pace is best."

After the boys had paddled for ten minutes the stream began to wander and the water plants became thicker. In the glow of moonlight Denny could see the spiky white flowers and round, flat leaves of water lilies.

Rick remarked, "A frog could cross this stream on lily pads without getting his feet wet."

The stream was shallower, too. With every stroke Denny's paddle hit the silty bottom.

Again Rick's voice came through the stillness. "We ought to have poles here to push ourselves along."

"Was it like this when you and your father came through?"

"No. The water was higher, I suppose because it was earlier in the summer."

Just as Rick spoke, the canoe came to a sudden stop.

"We're stuck on something!" said Denny.

Rick explored the water with his paddle. "Feels like a log. Push hard with your paddle."

"I am!"

"Come on. Both together. Rock forward and back. Don't tip us over in this muck, though. This isn't a boat, y'know."

As they struggled to get across the log a beam of light struck the canoe.

"What's that?" asked Rick in a hoarse whisper.

Denny glanced to the left. "Headlights from a car. That's the road over there."

"That close? We've been on this crazy stream for half an hour.

"Look for yourself," said Denny. "Here comes another car."

Again the headlights swept across the canoe and the two boys.

"That's bad," said Rick, pushing frantically with his paddle. "I'd forgotten this stream followed the road. A man with a rifle could pick us off like sitting ducks."

The Island in Fork Lake

Denny said crossly, "You're too jumpy. How would Leach know you're out here in the middle of this bog?"

Rick gave a forceful push with his paddle and they floated free.

"Denny," he said, "you don't know Leach. He's got it in for me and he'd follow me to the end of the earth."

"Where would he get the money to come up here looking for you? He'd have to have a car and money for food."

"He has money, plenty of it," said Rick. "He peddled dope, for one thing. Didn't use it himself, but he got a lot of kids hooked on the stuff and they'd steal or anything to buy from him."

"What a sweet guy!" remarked Denny. "What did you do to get him so mad?"

Rick paddled a few strokes before he answered. When he spoke his voice was full of emotion. "Leach killed a friend of mine. I saw him do it, and I told the police about it. When he came up to trial I testified against him."

Denny sat motionless, digesting this new information. "You said he escaped when he was being changed from one jail to another."

"Right."

"So he was convicted."

"Yes. It took forever. You know how trials hang on. He had a good lawyer who fought it all the way. If it weren't for my testimony he might've gone free — or at least gotten a lighter sentence. My friend who called to warn me said Leach has escaped with just one thing in mind. To get even with me."

"Oh, man! No wonder you left town in a

hurry." Automatically, Denny began to paddle again. "But Rick," he went on, "Algonquin's a big park. Leach won't know where to look for you here."

Rick said gloomily, "There's just the one road through the park. All he has to do is find my car, and I'm sure one of his pals has given him a description of it. I have a feeling his gang keeps track of me."

Denny began to feel less sure of their safety. "Yeah," he agreed. "A red Volkswagen with New York plates would be easy to spot and if he sees it he'll know we're someplace nearby."

"Well, I hid it the best I could," said Rick. "I drove back behind some bushes. And there's one good thing, Leach grew up in the city. He doesn't know a thing about canoes or the woods, so hopefully he'd have trouble following us."

"Through this bog he'd have trouble," agreed Denny.

"Anyway, let's forget Leach for now and keep our minds on making it through the stream. Don't get us hung up on any more logs."

"I can't see anything in this water. When I look down all I see is black."

"You have a better chance than I do. At least you're in front. Poke your paddle in the water ahead of you."

Denny grumbled, "Do you want me to paddle or poke the water? I can't do both."

They had been following the stream for more than an hour when Denny exclaimed, "There's open water ahead!"

Minutes later they pulled into a lake with water as still as glass.

Denny paddled with new power, enjoying the ease with which the canoe swished through the water. It was a relief to be free from logs and lily pads.

"You're doing well for a beginner," Rick complimented him. "You sure you've never been in a canoe before?"

"This is my first time. Honest."

Rick said, "This is Norway Lake. If I remember right, after we go across it we come to an outlet that connects with Fork Lake."

"Why not camp here?" asked Denny, peering toward shore. "I see some open places."

"Fork Lake is even better. And it's farther from the road. Come on. The worst is over."

"I hate to think of going back up that stream again," said Denny.

It took only a few minutes to reach the inlet but to Denny's disappointment it was as choked with water plants as the stream had been.

Rick encouraged him, "It isn't far to Fork Lake."

"What's that ahead?" asked Denny. "There's something dark all the way across the water."

As they drew nearer Rick said, "It's a dam. A beaver dam. I don't remember that."

The beaver had built well. The water beyond the dam was two feet below the depth of the water above.

Denny had gone on the Beaver Pond Trail with Holly and her father and had learned how cleverly the beaver made dams to raise the level of water so it was deep enough for the underwater entrance to their lodges. Right now he wished they were less clever.

"Now what do we do?" he asked. It was the middle of the night and he was tired.

"We'll pull up onto the dam," Rick said. "Then you get out and steady the canoe while I climb out."

Denny heard the patience in Rick's voice and bit back his protest.

The dam was stronger than he had expected. It held firm while he and Rick stood on it and hauled the canoe across.

But when they got back into the canoe below the dam, the water was so shallow they could not move.

"We'll have to get out," said Rick.

Denny thrust his paddle into the mud and discovered that he could touch bottom. The silt had an unpleasant smell of decay. He hated to put his feet into that muck, but he had no choice. He took off his sneakers and rolled his dungarees as high as he could. When he stepped into the water he sank above his knees. Walking was difficult and he was glad he was barefooted for the mud sucked at his feet with every step. He would have lost his sneakers.

"I think it will float now," said Rick, after ten minutes of wading and towing the canoe.

When he was back in the canoe Denny felt something on his leg. Exploring with his hand he touched a soft wormlike creature that clung to his skin.

He tried to pull it off but it would not let go.

"What are you doing?" asked Rick. "You're rocking the canoe."

"I've got something on my leg! I think it's a leech!" He scratched furiously at the creature and when it finally came loose it left his leg and hand wet and sticky.

"Ha!" said Rick. "Don't use that word *leech*!"

Denny fumbled in the dark for the flashlight and beamed it on his leg. "Go ahead and laugh. It isn't funny, though. I'm all bloody. That leech must've tapped an artery."

"What a baby you are! Doctors used to put leeches on people on purpose to bleed them," Rick said. "They thought it was good for what ailed you."

"I can picture the doctor opening his little black bag full of bloodsuckers! He wouldn't get near me." The canoe lurched to one side as Denny scooped up a handful of water to splash onto his leg.

"If you don't sit still we'll be in the muck again," growled Rick. "You probably picked up that leech in the mud. It's the kind of place they live."

The moon still showed the way as they entered Fork Lake.

Rick steered to the right. "We'll camp the same place Dad and I did, on an island. That was a year ago, but I'm sure I can find it."

A few minutes later the island loomed up ahead of them. It was not large, but as they drew nearer Denny could see a rocky shore backed by tall pines. Where on that dark island would they sleep?

As if he had read Denny's mind, Rick said, "The best camping place is at the other end, on the south side."

They landed on a sandy beach and Denny jumped out first to pull the canoe higher onto the shore.

The moon shed an eerie light on the narrow beach and the rocky point of land that jutted into the lake on the east. To the west the land was high with solid rock on the waterfront, backed by low bushes.

Rick led the way up the western slope. "Guess not many people come this way. Look here." He shone his light onto the ground. "This is the best place for a tent and it's all overgrown with blueberry bushes. That's good. They'll act like bedsprings under our sleeping bags.

They had the tent in place and Rick was already in his sleeping bag when Denny realized how hungry he was.

"Hey, Rick," he said. "I'm starved."

Rick yawned. "Help yourself. You know where I hung the food bag."

"You'd better get it,' 'said Denny. "I'm not sure I can reach it."

Rick raised his head. "Just like I said, you're a spoiled brat. You expect someone else to wait on you." He lay down again. "If you're hungry you'll find out how to get the food."

Denny crawled out of the tent feeling annoyed with himself for giving Rick another excuse for criticizing him.

With the help of his flashlight he found the tree where the food bag was hung, but it dangled from a branch high in the air above his head. Rick had tied the bag to one end of a rope. The other end of the rope was fastened around the trunk of the tree.

To his surprise, Denny found it was easy to untie the rope from the tree trunk and lower the bag. After a satisfying snack of dried fruit and cookies and a drink of water from the canteen, he felt pleased with himself until he found he couldn't get the bag into the air again. The rope that had held it had slid off the branch.

He wished he had seen how Rick had done it in the first place. He found it impossible to throw the rope over the branch, especially in the darkness.

Why bother? he thought wearily. This was an island. No bears would be here.

Finally he found a dead fir tree. Reaching as high as he could, he thrust the handles of the food bag over one of the bare branches.

When he crawled back into the tent, Rick mumbled, "Did you hang up the food bag?"

"Yes," answered Denny.

It wasn't a lie, he told himself. Rick hadn't asked where he had hung it.

The Night Visitor

Denny was awakened by soft noises outside the tent. He lay rigid, listening.

Bushes rustled. Twigs snapped. There was a sound of shuffling footsteps.

At once Denny thought of Leach. He had followed them and was fumbling around in the dark, looking for Rick! At any moment he would find their tent and that would be the end.

Quietly he inched down the zipper of his sleeping bag and slid nearer to Rick.

Putting his mouth next to his stepbrother's ear, he whispered, "Don't say anything. Listen."

Rick drew in a startled breath, but he did not speak.

The rustling steps came closer, then went away. Now Denny could hear a scratching noise and a series of grunts.

Rick whispered, "A bear. Must be looking for food. Good thing he can't get our food bag." He turned his head sharply toward Denny. "Or can he?"

"He might," admitted Denny. "I hung it on a lower branch."

Rick scrambled out of his sleeping bag and crawled to the front of the tent.

Denny followed him and peered over his shoulder. The moon, low in the western sky, still gave a pale light, enough so Denny could see the movement of a dark shape. Suddenly the shape rose up beside a tree.

It was a bear, all right, a huge one, and it was after the bag which Denny had hung on the branch. While the two boys watched, the animal reached up and cuffed the food bag. It fell to the ground with a thud and the bear dropped to all fours to investigate it.

Rick crawled back into the tent. He pulled on his shoes and seized his flashlight. Denny, tying his own wet sneakers, saw Rick beam his flashlight on the bear.

The animal lifted his head and backed away a few paces, dragging the food bag with him.

"Doggone him! We need that food!" said Rick under his breath.

All of their food was in the bag, as Denny knew well. And he had practically handed it to the bear. Rick would have good reason to be angry with him now. Desperation made Denny search earnestly for a way out of this new trouble.

They couldn't take the bag away from the bear. That would be suicide, he knew. Black bears weren't as dangerous as the grizzlies out west, but they could be deadly if they were angry. The thing to do was frighten him away.

What would frighten a bear? The flashlight hadn't bothered him much.

An idea came to Denny. Noise. He might be frightened away by loud noise.

"Rick!" he whispered. "Where are the cooking pans?"

Rick seemed to understand. Without a word he reached back and opened one of the pack-sacks. He pulled out the cook kit and a bag of eating utensils. Each boy took a pan and a large spoon.

"One, two, three!" counted Rick.

At *three* Rick and Denny began to beat on the pans with the spoons. The bear raised onto his hind legs, looking in their direction. Then he dropped to all fours and shuffled away, dragging the food bag.

The boys stepped out of the tent and continued to bang the pans and shout.

The noise was too much for the bear. He abandoned the bag and ran into the woods.

Rick darted after him and snatched up the bag of food. He showed Denny the hole made in it by the bear.

"A minute later and he'd have had it open," he said. "Already he's fixed it so it's no good if it rains. Won't keep bugs out, either. Oh, well. It'll have to do."

Going back to the tree where he had first hung the bag, Rick took up the loose end of rope from the ground. This he tied around a large stone which he then tossed over the tree branch.

"Oh, that's how you do it!" exclaimed Denny. He was waiting for Rick to explode about his leaving the food bag where a bear could reach it.

When the explosion did not come, Denny tried to explain. "I didn't think there'd be any bears on an island."

"They can swim, you know," replied Rick. "Don't try to alibi out of it, Denny. Admit you didn't have the guts to tell me you couldn't get the bag up in the air again."

"I didn't want to wake you up!"

"Come on, let's go back to bed." Rick sounded disgusted. "It's only 4:00 A.M. and I'm still beat."

But after the excitement of chasing the bear, Denny could not sleep. At first he lay awake listening for the shuffle of the bear's feet. Then as the silence continued he mulled over Rick's remark about his lack of guts.

He should talk about guts! thought Denny indignantly. He's running away from Leach. If he's so brave he should go back to Buffalo and have it out with him.

Leach was still a puzzle to Denny, a jigsaw puzzle with half the pieces missing.

Rick turned over restlessly. After a while he gave a deep sigh and turned over again.

Finally, Denny whispered, "Are you awake?"

Rick answered in a stage whisper, "Yes, I keep listening for that bear — or Leach."

"Me, too." Denny spoke in a normal tone. "Say, Rick, how come Leach killed your friend? Or was it an accident?"

"It was no accident," said Rick. "For one thing, it was a gang fight and they were in different gangs."

"A gang fight?" repeated Denny. "Were you in a gang?"

"No — not exactly. Forget it! I don't want to talk about it."

Denny was impatient. "You keep telling me a little and then you leave me in the air. You brought me along on this trip and I think you owe it to me to clue me in on the whole thing."

"I didn't mean to tell you anything, to begin with. You've just wormed it out of me."

"Why don't you want me to know?"

Rick said flatly, "I don't care if you know, but I don't want your mother to get the wrong idea about me. If she knew I'd had anything to do with a street gang she — she might not understand."

"All right. I won't tell my mother. I don't tell her everything."

Rick grunted. "I suppose you don't. Well —

you know this much. You might as well know the rest and maybe you'll stop pestering me."

"Start at the beginning," prompted Denny. He stretched out on his back in the sleeping bag, eager to hear the remainder of Rick's story. As he waited he was aware of the lap of waves on the shore.

"We used to live in Cleveland," Rick began.

"I know. So did we. Your father and my mother went to high school together."

"Shut up," said Rick, but his tone was good-natured. "I'm telling the story. Like I said, we were living in Cleveland and then about three years ago Dad got an offer of a better job in Buffalo. So he went there to start work and Mom and I stayed in Cleveland so she could sell the house and I could finish my school year. I was in ninth grade then."

Rick drew a deep breath. "Only nobody wanted to buy the house and after about six months Mom told Dad she wanted a divorce. While he was in Buffalo she met somebody she liked better."

"Oh, golly!" exclaimed Denny.

"Yeah," said Rick. His voice was carefully unemotional. "Well, when they split up I could take my choice, so I went with Dad. We lived in a dinky little apartment in downtown

Buffalo. And man! I was lonesome. All my friends were back in Cleveland and I didn't know a soul."

"Bad," said Denny with feeling. "That's the way it's been with me this past month."

Rick turned his head toward Denny, "Hey, Denny. That's right! And I haven't been much help."

"Forget it. Go on."

Rick said, "The worst of it was school. I had to go to a big downtown high school. I guess it was the roughest in the city. I'd go in the cafeteria and eat my lunch alone. I couldn't seem to strike up a friendship with anyone."

Denny muttered, "I hate eating alone."

Rick went on, "Then one day this kid named Frank came over and sat down at the table where I was eating and he began talking to me. I was so glad to see that guy I'd have given him my right hand if he'd asked for it." Rick sat up and hugged his knees.

"We hung around together after that," he said. "And I felt good because I wasn't alone anymore. After school he'd come over to the apartment and sometimes I went home with him. It wasn't much of a house where he lived, but it was decent. His mother and father both worked and Frank had a brother a year younger than he was and two little sisters."

Denny was puzzled. "If you liked Frank so much how come you never talked about him before? I've been with you for a month and you never mentioned him and he hasn't been over to the house."

Rick sighed in the darkness. "You won't see Frank. He's dead. He's the one Leach killed."

"Oh!" Denny was shocked. "And you saw him do it!"

Rick nodded.

Eye Witness

"That must have been really rough, seeing your friend killed like that," said Denny. He thought over what Rick had told him. "You said it was a gang fight. Did your friend Frank belong to a gang?"

Rick lay down again. "Yeah. Growing up in a tough neighborhood like he did, he could hardly help it. The kids in the gang were from his street. You know, neighborhood kids. They were a wild bunch and I didn't like them much. But Frank liked to hang around with them, so I went along — three times." He drew in a deep breath before he went on.

"They used to get together in the evening and rap and kid around and look at the people going by. Frank said sometimes they snatched purses or did some shoplifting. I guess they got into a lot of devilment, but I never saw any of that action.

"The third time I went with them," continued Rick, "we were standing around in an alley behind some stores. There weren't many people around and there wasn't anything to do. Some of the gang were wrestling and some others were shooting dice.

"Then all at once a couple of old cars pulled up and a mob of fellows jumped out and pitched into Frank's gang. Seems they were enemies from way back.

"One big fellow with a lot of curly hair — brown hair — started toward Frank and me and I saw he had a knife. He looked about eighteen. Frank saw him, too, and he said, 'That's Leach. Don't tangle with him.'

"I stood there like a dummy and Frank

gave me a shove and I landed in a bunch of cartons that were out for garbage collection."

Now that Rick had started talking, the words poured out of him.

"I was getting out of the pile of cartons," he said, "when I saw Leach make a dive for Frank. He had that knife and he brought it down hard in Frank's chest. You never saw anything so fast. Frank fell down and lay still. Then Leach saw that I was watching and I thought I was next. But one of his gang grabbed Leach and said something to him. They all got back in the cars and left. Frank's gang faded, too. I was surprised they went off and left him.

"I went over to him," continued Rick. "There was blood on his shirt and I'm pretty sure he was dead already. I wondered if it was partly because of me that he was dead. Maybe he'd have gotten away if he hadn't stopped to make sure I was clear of Leach.

"I was there on my knees beside him when a police car came up. I suppose that's why the others all left. They heard the sirens. I was too worried about what was going on in the alley to hear anything else."

"Wow!" said Denny softly. "Did the police think you had killed Frank?"

"I guess not. I was crying and telling them to get Frank to a hospital. I suppose they could see he was my friend and I wouldn't hurt him. They called an ambulance. Then they asked me what happened and I told them the whole thing. I gave them a good description of Leach."

"And Leach found out you put the finger on him, so that's why he wants to kill you. To get even, you said."

"Right," said Rick. "I'm sure he'd have gotten me long before this, but the police picked him up and held him without bail."

"You still didn't tell me why he killed Frank. Must've had some reason."

"He did. Same reason he wants to wipe me out. For revenge. Frank's kid brother, Gus, clued me in afterward." Rick sounded grim. "I told you Leach was pushing drugs. At first it was pot and pills. Then he got hold of some heroin and got one of Frank's friends hooked on it. That's bad stuff, y'know, and when Frank saw what it did to his pal, he started a one-man campaign against buying from Leach."

"Oh. So that cut down on Leach's sales."

"Like crazy."

The picture of Leach in Denny's mind was becoming more ugly by the minute.

"Did you have to go to court when they had the trial?" he asked.

"Sure. I was the chief witness against Leach." Rick shuddered. "I can feel him glaring at me there in the courtroom. Anyway, he was convicted and sentenced. When he was sent off to jail I thought that was the last I'd hear of him. Then Gus — Frank's brother — phoned and told me Leach had escaped and was after me."

"So Gus was the one who phoned you that night we left home," said Denny. "Say, how come I never heard about this gang fight and Frank getting killed? I'd think it would've been in all the papers and on TV."

"It was, around Buffalo, but of course you were in Cleveland. My name was never mentioned, though. Guess I was lucky. Or maybe it was because I was underage then. I was only fifteen."

"So my mother doesn't know," said Denny.

"That's right. And I hope she'll never find out. Dad doesn't want anyone to know. He was afraid I'd get a reputation for being involved with a gang murder. He said that could haunt me the rest of my life."

Denny considered this. "I don't see why. You weren't fighting. You didn't even belong to a gang."

"Well, whatever," said Rick. "That's one reason I came up here instead of going to the police. I told you I didn't call them because I panicked. Well, I did panic all right but I wouldn't have gone to the police anyway. If a reporter knew Leach was chasing me he'd soon find out why and the whole thing would be in the news. I'm not a juvenile anymore."

"I can see why you want to keep it from the newspapers," conceded Denny. "But you're all wrong about my mother. You don't know her as well as I do. She'd understand about Leach and the gang better than you think."

"You sure?"

"I'm positive Mom wouldn't blame you. What about Aunt Wilma? Does she know?"

"Yeah. You can't keep anything from Aunt Wilma," said Rick.

Denny asked, "Do you ever see any of the gang anymore?"

"No. Well, I keep in touch with Gus. He's grateful to me because I stood by Frank."

"That took nerve," admitted Denny. He wondered if he would be brave enough to stand by a friend like that. Probably not, he thought ruefully, when he didn't even have the guts to tell Rick he couldn't hang up the food bag.

106

Rick chuckled to himself. "Something good came out of all that trouble. Dad took me to Algonquin last summer because he thought if he had spent more time with me I wouldn't have gotten mixed up with Frank's gang. We had a swell time and did a lot of talking. He even opened up some about Mom. Did both of us good."

Denny was stunned by Rick's story. But he could understand a little better why Rick had run away from Leach instead of going to the cops.

Rick climbed out of his sleeping bag. "I'm getting up. No use staying in the sack when I can't sleep. Might as well get breakfast."

He started a fire and soon the smell of frying bacon mingled with the scent of the pines and the fishy smell of the beach.

When they had finished eating, Rick said, "I got the breakfast so you can clean up."

"Right," said Denny, trying to sound confident, but when he looked at the greasy frying pan, the cocoa cups, and eating utensils, he did not know where to start.

Rick seemed to read his mind. "You wash the dishes in one of the cooking pans. There's hot water in the pan on the fire and soap in that plastic bag over there."

Denny was glad when his stepbrother went

to the tent and left him alone to the struggle with his unaccustomed task. He still had not finished when Rick came back half an hour later carrying his fishing pole.

"I'm going to try my luck," he said. "Ought to be lots of fish in this lake."

"I want to fish, too."

Rick laid his pole on a rock. "OK. Finish the dishes and I'll fix a pole for you."

By the time he came back with another pole, Denny was ready to go. The clean dishes and pans were packed away and he had put out the fire. He hoped for a word of praise but Rick said nothing about the neat cooking area.

"Did you ever go fishing?" he asked.

"No," Denny admitted.

"Did you ever do *anything* except watch TV?"

Denny was hurt. "I played trumpet in the school band. And I'm pretty good at photography. I swim and play football. What do you want?"

"Football! A shrimp like you?"

Denny defended himself. "I wasn't on a regular team. Just a lot of us kids got together. I'm better than you think, though. I'm a fast runner and a pretty good tackle."

"Sorry." Rick held out a small plastic box. "Pick out a plug you want to use. We don't have any worms so we'll see how the Algonquin fish like these artificial lures."

Denny chose a lure that looked like a minnow. Several small hooks dangled from its belly.

As it turned out, the fish were especially attracted to the plastic minnow. Denny was awkward at casting; his line got tangled in bushes along the shore. But by the end of the morning he had three large black bass. Rick had only one because he had done most of the paddling.

"Beginner's luck," he said with a grin. "You caught 'em, you clean 'em."

Again Denny had to be taught, but he tackled the job without complaining. As he sat beside the lake, scraping scales from his fish, a feeling of contentment swept over him.

"I could go for this life," he commented.

Rick had finished cleaning his one fish and was sitting on a rock nearby.

"Sometimes I have hopes for you, Denny," he said. "You may turn into a useful human being some day." He added with a smile, "Yeah, it's great here, even if I do have to worry about Leach. But there's someone else

I wish were here. No offense to you, of course."

"Who's that?"

"Beth."

Denny said morosely, "I wouldn't mind if Holly were here, myself, but I'll never see her again. I'm glad I took her picture. At least I'll have that."

"You really liked that girl, didn't you?" said Rick. "Be too bad if you lost track of her. I think I know a way we can get her address. They must have it at the Mew Lake office. I had to give my name and address. So Mr. Adams must've given his. We'll stop on the way home and ask."

Denny felt happiness spread through his whole body. He had not lost Holly, after all.

The Wolves Answer

Early that afternoon Rick and Denny had a reminder that they were not far from civilization when a pontoon plane flew over the lake. It was a yellow, single-engine plane with black markings on the side.

As it approached, Rick dashed to the shelter of the woods, but Denny, who was coming in from a swim, waved at it. The little plane dipped its wings and circled back to the north.

"Come on out!" Denny called. "That's a government plane. You don't have to worry about that kind. They fly over the park all the time looking for fires or people who need help."

Rick emerged from the woods. "You sure learned a lot about this park in one day."

"Holly and her father are good teachers." Denny flopped down on the sandy beach. "That plane was a Beaver. There's another kind, a larger plane they use, that's called an Otter."

Rick frowned. "There's no reason why a government plane can't be looking for us. Say Leach makes up some story about why he wants to find us. He describes me and the canoe. Then when the pilot comes back with his report, Leach rents a canoe and comes after me."

"In here?" scoffed Denny. He stretched out on his stomach, enjoying the heat of the sun on his wet back. "You said Leach doesn't know anything about the wilderness. He'd never make it down that stream."

Rick said gloomily, "He'd find a way. Seeing that plane makes me realize how easy it would be to locate us. How can we hide from planes?" Rick slumped onto the ledge of rock above the lake.

Denny argued, "Plane or no plane, Leach still doesn't know how to handle a canoe."

Rick put his head in his hands. "Don't expect me to make sense. I think one thing one minute and something else the next."

Denny felt sorry for him. "Cool it. We're going to get out of this OK."

"Thanks. I hope you're right. But Denny, that guy's real trouble!" Rick flung a stone into the lake. It splashed far out from shore. "I wonder what made him that way? Huh? His folks never came to court. Maybe they never were there when he needed them. But no matter what caused it, he's danger now."

Denny listened with sympathy, but he could not think of anything to say.

Rick rubbed his hand over his chin. "I think I won't shave. If I have a beard maybe Leach won't recognize me. What do you think?"

Denny stood up and stretched luxuriously. "Just shave it off before you see Beth."

"I don't know," said Rick. "She might think I look cool with whiskers."

"Forget the whiskers!" cried Denny. He pointed to the northeast where a peninsula jutted from the island into the lake. There on the shore was a large black animal. "Isn't that a bear?"

Rick jumped up. "It is!"

The bear waded into the water up to its shoulders and began to swim toward the mainland.

Denny raced to the tent for his camera.

"Hurry up!" called Rick. "He's halfway across already."

"Keep track of him while I get this telephoto on," begged Denny.

He quickly checked the adjustments and was in time for one shot of the bear swimming with only its head above water.

Then, keeping the bear in focus, Denny took another picture as the animal climbed out of the water and onto the rocky shore.

The bear, unconscious of being watched, shook itself like a dog and then walked toward the woods, stopping to sniff at something among the rocks.

"Must be the bear who tried to make off with our food bag," remarked Rick. "Good riddance. But of course it can swim back again tonight."

He watched Denny adjusting his camera. "You seem to be pretty good with that. You going to be a photographer?"

Denny continued to follow the bear through the viewfinder. "I dunno. I only like to take outdoor pictures."

"You could be a photo-journalist," suggested Rick. "Travel all over the world and take pictures of things and write articles about them."

"Sounds good." Denny took one last picture of the bear before it blended into the shadows among the trees. "Mr. Adams says we should be afraid of bears but not of wolves," Denny said. "But whether I'm a photo-journalist or not, the only way I'll ever hunt is with a camera."

Rick began to gather driftwood for the evening fire. "What about hunting for food? I think it's OK to kill deer if you're going to eat them. Some animals get too plentiful if they're not hunted, and then they starve."

"It may be all right," Denny conceded. "But I'm not going to hunt. Mr. Adams says everything in nature has a place of its own and it took millions of years to work it all out. He says plants and animals and everything have their own jobs and if one kind of animal or bird or insect is wiped out, that upsets the balance. Like a pile of blocks. If you pull out one block the whole stack comes down."

"What about things like rattlesnakes?"

"They have a place, too," Denny insisted. "Even mosquitoes and black flies are important. They help to feed the birds."

Rick laughed. "You've been brainwashed."

"Maybe. But what Mr. Adams says makes sense."

"You're right," Rick agreed soberly. "I was just pulling your leg. I go along with conservation, too. Except I do plan to go hunting some time. You know what made me see the light about protecting our environment? The pictures the astronauts took of the world. Man, it looked like the globes of the earth we had at school — only more — shiny and alive. And it looked so alone, surrounded by all that space. I thought, When that's gone, there isn't any more. Not for us."

Denny grinned. "When I saw those pictures I thought, Columbus was right. The earth *is* round."

They were cooking dinner when another plane came in low and fast from the north. They did not hear or see it until it was almost overhead. This time Rick didn't have time to run to the woods.

"That's a private plane!" he exclaimed, crouching among the rocks.

The aircraft disappeared among the clouds to the south but it came back again a few minutes later, still flying low. It went directly over the island at a slow speed. Even Denny felt uneasy, and Rick covered his head with his arms.

"Well, they certainly got a good look at us!" grumbled Rick. "I don't like it at all!"

Denny tried to reassure him. "It could be somebody trying to find a good lake to fish in or just taking in the scenery."

Rick refused to be cheered up. "I think it's Leach. He found my car and figured out I'd have to be nearby. Then he hired a plane to take him around to look for me."

"If Leach was in that plane it would have landed," said Denny.

"Uh, uh," objected Rick. "Private planes can't land on the park lakes, except in certain places, and this isn't one of the places. Besides, I don't think Leach would land, anyway. He couldn't walk up and kill me with the pilot of the plane watching." Rick paced up and down the beach. "No. He'll be back later by canoe, just as I told you."

When they had eaten, Rick went to the tent. He returned with a map of eastern Canada which he studied as if it were a lesson he had to memorize.

Darkness came early because of the heavy clouds. The air was hot and still and there were more mosquitoes than before.

Denny toasted a marshmallow over the coals of the campfire and then browned another to take to Rick who was sitting on a rock on the west side of the island.

"Man, it's dark!" said Denny as he held out the marshmallow.

Rick pulled the candy from the stick and popped it it into his mouth. "Thanks. Yeah," he mumbled, "can't even see the other shore."

Denny knew his stepbrother was listening and watching for Leach, but he decided not to bring up the subject. As he stood there staring into the darkness, he thought of the night of the wolf howl. The naturalist, Mr. Kosac, had said there were packs of wolves scattered all over the park. There might even be some wolves over there to the west across that narrow strip of water.

Without any forethought, Denny lifted his head and let out a wolf howl. He was surprised at how realistic it sounded.

Rick jumped up and shook him. "You idiot! Are you trying to tell Leach where we are?"

Denny pulled away. "You're the dope! He isn't looking for a wolf."

Before Rick had time to answer, a sound came from the northwest, in the direction of the road. It was an eerie, hair-raising sound, the howl of a pack of wolves.

Denny was pleased and excited. "They answered me! What d'you know!"

Rick said sarcastically, "I suppose they'll come over to call on us tonight."

"That would be swell," said Denny, unruffled. "But they won't come. They're very shy animals."

"Yeah. And it could be that wasn't any animal who answered you."

"You think it was some person, like maybe Leach?"

"Right."

"No way," said Denny. "That was several wolves. Didn't you hear that? More like a male and female wolf and a couple of young ones, just learning to howl. Mr. Kosac played a record like that. The cubs have higher voices than the old wolves. They were the ones that were yipping and whining."

Rick groaned. "You and your wolves. Why don't you go to bed?"

"Are you going to sit out here all night?"

"I may."

"Are you waiting for Leach?"

"Yes."

"What if you do see him? What good will it do?"

"At least he won't stab me in the back while I sleep." He stood up and stretched. "You'd better turn in, Denny. I may decide to leave here — maybe go on through the park and up into Quebec."

"Do we have enough money for that?"

"It's tight. But I'm not going to sit here and wait for Leach. I'm positive he was in that plane this afternoon." Rick sat down again on the rock. "Go on to bed. You didn't get much sleep last night. If you don't get some rest you won't be any help. You'll go to sleep with the paddle in your hand."

"What about you, Superman?"

"Well, I'm about beat, I admit. But sleep's out of the question. You can't understand, and I hope you never will, what it's like to know there's a knife or a bullet with your name on it."

"What about soldiers on the battlefront? They have to sleep."

"I know it. I don't see how they do."

"I think we ought to go home. Anyway, you

could be scared in comfort in your own bed."

"Forget it," said Rick. "Leach would call his pals and they'd tell him I was back in town. He'd find me in no time. At least up here there are a lot of places to hide."

"Look," Denny argued. "You could tell the immigration officers at the U.S. end of the bridge that Leach would be coming, and they'd stop him and that would be the end of him. He'd be in prison with a longer sentence than before."

"I wish I could believe that, but I can't." Rick turned his back on Denny and gazed steadily toward the north.

Denny gave up and headed for the tent, waving his hands around his head to fend off the mosquitoes that were more plentiful away from the waterfront.

The air inside the tent was heavy and Denny thought of pulling his sleeping bag outside. However, he decided heat was better than mosquitoes.

He sprawled on top of the two sleeping bags, dressed only in his undershorts. It would be impossible to sleep, he thought. It was too hot in here, and anyway, it was only eight-thirty, for Pete's sake!

He awoke to find Rick shaking him.

"It's about time you came to!" exclaimed Rick. "I've packed everything, including my sleeping bag. I pulled it out from under you and you kept right on sleeping."

Denny looked around, still in a daze. Rick's glowing flashlight made the tent like the inside of a cave. "Is it morning already?"

"In a way. It's twelve-thirty."

"Why'd you wake me up?"

"Because we're leaving," said Rick. "I've decided to take your advice. We're going home."

Retreat from the Island

Home! The word sounded good to Denny. Camping was fun, but not with Rick acting so jumpy.

He pulled on his shirt and dungarees, shivering in the cool air. Now that he was wide awake he was surprised to find out he felt rested even though it still was the middle of the night.

When he crawled out of the tent he found that a breeze had come up, blowing away the heat and mosquitoes of the evening before. Only a few clouds remained in the sky and the full moon which had been hidden when he went to sleep was shining brightly overhead.

Rick was pulling up tent stakes. Denny hastily snatched his sleeping bag out of the sagging tent and thrust it into a backpack. Then he helped Rick with the tent.

"Did you go to sleep?" he asked.

"Yeah," said Rick sheepishly. "Right after you left I stretched out on the ground to rest and I fell asleep. I woke up only a few minutes ago." He yawned. "Now I know how soldiers can sleep."

Rick tied a rope around the tent stakes. "When I saw the moon I decided we might as well get started. I have a strong hunch that Leach will come in here as soon as it's daylight."

"But you said he doesn't know anything about the woods or boats. How could he paddle a canoe in here when the two of us had such a hard time?"

Rick rolled the tent, stakes, and poles together in a tight bundle. "If Leach saw us yesterday — and I'm sure he was in that

124

plane — he'll find a way to get in here. He's desperate. He knows he's going to get caught sooner or later and he's determined to get me while he's on the loose. It doesn't bother him any to take chances. He's already up for murder." Rick handed Denny a flashlight. "Check the ground to see if we left anything and then come down to the canoe."

When Denny reached the shore Rick had the canoe packed.

"Got something for you," he said. He handed Denny a small plastic bag which contained a thick wedge of cheese between two slices of bread.

"Hey, thanks!" said Denny. "How'd you know I was hungry?"

"How do I know a cat has kittens? Eat it while you paddle. Let's go."

Denny pushed the canoe off the sand and, feeling quite expert, he gave a final shove with one foot as he stepped into the bow.

As soon as he was seated, he took a large bite of the sandwich and laid the rest of it on the seat beside him while he and Rick back-paddled away from shore. The cheese and bread were good and he had the contented feeling that usually came with eating.

It sure was nice of Rick to fix him a sandwich, he thought. Things had been going better between Rick and him lately. Maybe they were going to be like real brothers, after all.

Denny looked back at the island, rising from the water like a dark ship. It seemed as if they had been there longer than a day and part of a night. He had done things on the island he had never tried before — catching fish and cleaning them, building a fire, scaring off a bear, and howling at the wolves. Perhaps that was why he felt so much older.

He hoped they could come back again when they could enjoy camping without worrying about Leach.

Denny snatched another bite of the sandwich and then bent to paddle vigorously. It was surprising to him how easy it was to see tonight. The lake acted like a huge mirror, reflecting the light from the moon.

Not far ahead on the left he could see the break in the shoreline where the inlet entered the lake. In a few hours they would be home. Rick would report to the police the way he should have done right at the start, and everything would be the same as before the phone call that had started them on this trip.

Denny wondered why all at once he had a let-down feeling. Perhaps he wasn't ready to go back to sitting in front of the TV. I'm through hanging around the house, he decided. I'm going to go out on my bike and take my camera along. There must be some interesting things to photograph not too far away.

"Hey, Rick. Can we stop at Mew Lake to get Holly's address?" he asked.

"With any luck we'll be out of the park before the office opens at the campground. We'll write for the address."

Denny was disappointed, but he did not argue. It was more important right now to get Rick away from Leach. *If* Leach were really after him. Denny still had his doubts that a tough criminal would go to so much trouble to do away with his stepbrother.

Rick spoke up. "I've been thinking about how Leach might get in here. He could hire a guide to paddle the canoe. His plan might be to kill me *and* the guide so there wouldn't be anyone to report on him."

"What about me?" asked Denny.

"Oh, yeah. He'd have to kill you, too."

"Great," said Danny. He began to peer ahead with more interest than before.

Rick went on. "It could be weeks before anyone would find the bodies. People don't come down this way. I'm glad we're getting out, even though it is beautiful. I feel trapped because I don't know of anywhere we can go from Fork Lake. There are other lakes beyond Fork, but there aren't any portage routes marked on the map I have and I'm not enough of a woodsman to blaze my own trail. I think this is kind of a dead end."

"Yuk!" said Denny. "Do you have to call it a *dead* end?"

The trip through the inlet was easier than it had been the night before. Now they were able to avoid some of the worst spots, and although they had to get out and tow the canoe through the shallows below the beaver dam, this time they did not pick up any leeches.

Shortly before they reached Norway Lake a large heron rose from the reeds ahead of them and flew with slow, heavy wings across the streak of moonlight in the water.

Denny felt the canoe jerk as Rick gave a startled jump.

"What's the matter?" asked Denny. "Did you think that was Leach hiding in the grass?"

Rick said moodily, "You needn't laugh. I keep expecting to meet him head on. Leach could've decided to travel by moonlight, too."

Denny was sorry he had teased his stepbrother. After all, he was uptight enough without having it rubbed in. But Rick's nervousness proved contagious. As they entered Norway Lake, Denny found himself looking anxiously into the shadows along the shore. Was that a canoe or only a floating log, overgrown with moss and bushes? Leaves, blown by a breeze, turned white faces to the moonlight, and all around the edge of the lake the white birch trees were narrow ghosts.

At last they reached the entrance to the creek that wound through the bog to the road. This winding stream was the hardest part of the entire trip. Denny's back and arms ached with the effort of helping to keep the canoe on course.

The wind that had cleared the sky had died down and again the clouds gathered. The moon, now in the west, seemed to slide in and out of the clouds. One moment Denny could see the path of open water between the clumps of water lilies, and the next moment there was only darkness and he didn't know which way to go.

To make matters worse, a squadron of mosquitoes arrived to escort the canoe. While the boys' hands were busy with the paddles, the mosquitoes settled to bite wherever they could find uncovered skin.

Now they were traveling parallel to the

road and they saw the headlights of an occasional car. At last during a moment when the moon broke free of clouds, Denny glimpsed the large culvert.

"Full steam ahead!" he said in relief.

Rick said softly, "Take it easy. We're getting into the most dangerous area. No telling where Leach is."

So without another word they approached the culvert. Still in silence they plunged into the darkness under the road where the sound of their paddles dipping into the water was amplified. Emerging from the other side of the culvert, the first thing that met Denny's eyes was a canoe against the righthand bank of the stream. He was glad to see that it was empty, but he heard his stepbrother draw in a sharp breath.

"I knew it!" whispered Rick. "Leach is ready for an early start!"

A Man of Fury

For a moment Rick and Denny sat motionless with their paddles in the air.

Denny finally tore his eyes away from the empty canoe long enough to glance from one side of the creek to the other. He feared that a man would rise out of the deep grass, but he saw no one.

He became aware that the canoe was traveling backward. His stepbrother was silently back-paddling through the culvert.

When they emerged into the moonlight on the other side, Rick whispered, "Did you see anyone?"

"No." Denny turned to look at him. "Are we going back to the island?"

"No. I'm trying to find a place to land."

Denny was horrified. "We can't get out of here!" He remembered too well how his paddle had sunk into the bottomless mud on this side of the culvert.

"Quiet!" breathed Rick. He paddled forward again, toward the culvert, and then tied the canoe to a bush on the left side of the stream.

A mass of huge boulders rose steeply from the water. Rick, first thrusting a flashlight into his pocket, climbed out and began to crawl over the rocks, keeping well below the road. He motioned for Denny to follow him.

Rock-climbing in semidarkness was not easy, Denny discovered, and with his short legs he was at a disadvantage. He saw Rick some distance ahead waiting and motioning for him to hurry.

When he caught up with his stepbrother,

Rick said, "You remember those two big rocks on either side of the path over there?"

"Yes." The sentinel rocks, he had called them to himself.

"We're about opposite them now. We'll climb up here and as soon as the coast is clear we'll run across the road and head straight for the woods. Then we'll circle around to the left toward the parking lot."

At the top of the bank they crouched, waiting while a car roared past. When Rick darted across, Denny followed close behind him. He had no wish to be alone in strange territory, especially when Leach might be in the vicinity.

The trees in the woods were small and the undergrowth was so heavy it was difficult to walk quietly. Every now and then Denny had to untangle himself from a bush. He guessed that few people walked through these woods, for often he felt the feathery touch of a cobweb on his face.

Rick was not using the flashlight but was feeling his way along. Denny could understand why. If Leach had seen them on the island it was quite likely that he was hiding nearby, planning to go to Fork Lake after them as soon as it was daylight. That is, if the canoe by the culvert was his.

133

Rick halted without warning and dropped to the ground. Denny crouched behind him wondering why they had stopped.

As he strained his eyes into the darkness, the moon made one of its appearances and a clearing came into view on the left. It must be the parking lot Rick had mentioned, for two cars were standing in it.

But Rick was not looking at the lot. He was facing straight ahead. Gradually Denny could make out the familiar shape of the VW, partially hidden by bushes, not more than three canoe-lengths away.

Why not go on? he wondered. He was about to speak to Rick when he saw the man.

He came from the woods on the far side of the VW and stood there, a great shadowy figure. Something was in his hand. A club of some kind. He raised it above his head and brought it down on the VW with an ear-splitting crash that was followed by a rain of glass.

Again the club came down. Again. And again. Denny was sure the windshield must be completely gone and perhaps some other windows, too.

Why doesn't Rick stop him? he wondered. But even as he wondered, he knew the answer. The man was Leach, and Rick wouldn't go near him for any reason. As he stared at the towering hulk, Denny could understand Rick's fear.

It wasn't just his size that was frightening. It was the fury of his attack on the VW. If he would do that to Rick's car, what would he do to Rick?

The man tossed the club into the woods and crouched down on the other side of the car. He was out of sight but Denny could hear a faint hissing sound. Leach was letting the air out of the tires! He was making sure they couldn't get away.

As soon as he had flattened all the tires, Leach strode out to the parking lot. It was then that Denny was able to get a fairly good look at the man. In the open lot he looked larger than ever. He walked with a kind of heavy grace, as if he were well coordinated.

I'll bet he can move fast, thought Denny, even if he is big.

But one thing puzzled him. Rick had said that Leach had curly brown hair. Of course the moonlight didn't show colors, but Denny was sure Leach's hair was not brown. It was light-colored. In the moonlight it shone like the pale flowers and dried grass along the road.

Leach climbed into one of the cars in the

parking lot. The moon again ducked behind a cloud, so Denny could not see the car clearly, but he heard it roll across the gravel, and then came the sound of the motor roaring away to the right.

Rick stood up. "Now you've — seen Leach." His voice shook slightly. "What do you think of him?"

"You're right, he looks like an ape. A good-looking ape," said Denny. "But what about his hair? He's a blond. Are you sure that's the right man?"

"I'm sure. He must've bleached his hair to disguise himself. He has a girl friend in Buffalo. Maybe she did it for him." Rick turned around. "We've got to move fast while he's gone. No telling when he'll be back." He glanced over his shoulder at Denny. "No doubt about it, now. Leach was in that plane that flew over the island."

Denny stared after his stepbrother. "Aren't you going to look at the car?"

Rick continued to walk away. "What's the use?"

That was true, Denny had to agree. "How are we going to get home if we can't drive the VW?"

"We aren't going home. We're going to pick up our duffel and walk to the next big lake. That's Opeongo. It can't be more than five miles."

"You're out of your mind!" cried Denny. "Let's get out in the road and hitch a ride to the nearest police station. If we tell the police about the car they might even catch Leach when he comes back to the parking lot."

Rick said angrily, "We're not hitching any ride. Wouldn't that be great to have Leach drive up and give us a lift — to the nearest cemetery!"

Denny stumbled after his stepbrother. Rick was as unreasonable now has he had been at the start of their trip. Leach seemed to scare the sense out of him.

"How are we going to carry the packs and the canoe five miles?" he demanded.

"We aren't going to take the canoe to Lake Opeongo." Rick did not slow down. "We're going to rent one when we get there. They have a store and a boat rental place."

"But what's to prevent Leach from flying over and finding us there?"

Rick paused briefly. "Denny, Opeongo is a big lake and it connects up with a chain of lakes. It'll be easy to drop out of sight. We should've gone there in the first place."

"We *ought* to go to the police!"

"OK, OK. There's a phone at Opeongo.

We'll call the police from there. Now come on. Don't be chicken."

Chicken — *me*, thought Denny angrily. He's the one who's chicken — he's running like a scared rabbit.

Rick came to a halt. "Here's where we cross the road. From here on there's no cover at all on this side."

Again they raced across and made their way painfully over the boulders to the canoe.

"Let's shove this canoe into the bog," said Rick. "If Leach doesn't see it he may waste some time going to Fort Lake looking for us."

Denny cautiously tested a clump of grass with one foot. When it yielded under his weight, he scrambled back onto the rocks.

Rick was already waist-deep in marsh grass. "Get in here and help me!" he snapped. "You won't sink out of sight." He added more gently, "This is firmer than the bottom of the stream."

Feeling angry but ashamed, Denny plunged into the bog. Rick was right, this was just swampy ground, not like quicksand.

They slid the canoe into the bog where the grass was high and then tossed handfuls of the long grass over it.

"I'm afraid it'll show from the road by daylight," worried Rick, "but I don't know what else we can do."

With sodden sneakers and dungarees wet above the knees, they climbed the rocks to the road, carrying the heavy packs and the food bag.

"Mom would have a fit if she saw me now," said Denny with a grin. "She always saying, 'Keep your feet dry!'"

Rick paused to adjust his pack. "All mothers say that, even mine."

Rick so rarely mentioned his own mother that Denny suspected that he still felt bitter because she had left him and Vince.

In a way, thought Denny, you might feel worse if your mother left you than if she died. It would keep eating at you and you'd wonder if you'd done anything that made her go away. Of course it wouldn't be your fault, but you'd wonder. And you'd want to see her and you couldn't.

At first the boys had no choice but to walk along the highway, for the bog stretched on either side, a steep ten feet below the road. If Leach came along now, they were done for, thought Denny.

As soon as possible, they crossed the road and entered the edge of the woods. Here the uneven ground and thick undergrowth made walking slow.

They soon gave up traveling in the woods, but even on the strip of cleared land beside the road the ground was uneven and they were constantly diving behind the trees to hide from cars. Every step of the way the pack was a crushing weight, and the air was warm and muggy.

After an hour of hiking Denny did not see how he could go on. His back and legs ached. Perspiration ran down his face in sticky streams. Mosquitoes buzzed around his head.

He stumbled on a stone and fell down. The ground felt good, so he stayed there.

Rick came back to him. "Did you get hurt?"

"I hurt all over."

"I mean did you sprain your ankle or something?"

"No."

"Then get up."

"I'm beat. I can't go another step. You go on."

Rick stood over him, silent. Then he said, "OK," turned on his heel, and trudged on.

Denny raised up and stared after him, unable to believe Rick would walk off and leave him.

Two cars rushed by, going west. Neither seemed to notice him.

Slowly Denny got to his feet. He felt better after his short rest, but he resented Rick's attitude.

I could stay here and die for all he cares, thought Denny. *It's the last time I'm going on a trip with him!*

Daylight came before they reached the lake but it was a gray, sullen light. The air was humid and still.

"We're in for a storm," muttered Rick. "I hope we can get a start up the lake before it hits. Could be a bad one after this heat."

"I'm phoning the police before we go anyplace," Denny reminded him.

"All right. Go ahead if it'll make you feel better."

A sign said LAKE OPEONGO, and they turned left onto a dirt road bordered by goldenrod, wild asters, and the white, clustered heads of pearly everlasting.

At last they reached the lake. A small store with a front porch that contained two rocking chairs was directly in front of them.

Down a slope to the right was a small building surrounded by rowboats and motorboats. By the shore were racks of canoes. Some were bright green and some were aluminum that shone like silver. Beside them a row of docks extended into the water like the teeth of a rake.

Denny's spirits lifted. In a place like this there was sure to be a pay phone. He set his pack onto the porch. After he had phoned he might even have a chance to sit on one of those rocking chairs.

Storm on Opeongo

Rick said, "Everything looks dead around here." He studied his watch. "Quarter before seven. Wonder what time they open up?"

When he went down the slope to the boat-rental office, Denny set out to find a telephone. He tried the store but that was locked.

Circling the building, he was startled to

come upon a man sitting on a bench behind the store. He was an Indian, Denny was sure. His hair was straight and as black as Rick's, and although he appeared young, his face had the leathery look of a man who was out in all weather.

"Morning," said the Indian. "Looks like we're in for a storm."

"I guess so," agreed Denny. He noticed that the man was carving something with a small, sharp knife.

"I *know* so. I've lived here all my life and the sky talks to me like a brother. That one up there — " he pointed with his knife at the dark sky, "tells me a thunderstorm's coming along with a big wind."

Denny had other things on his mind. "Is there a telephone around here?"

"There's one in the store, but that won't be open till seven o'clock. Might as well sit down here and wait."

Denny dropped onto the bench with a weary grunt. He wiped the perspiration from his face with his arm.

"What's your name, young fellow?" asked the Indian. "Mine's Jack."

"I'm Denny Mitchell." In spite of his fatigue, he had to smile. He had thought Indians were quiet, but this one was friendly and talkative.

Jack's brown eyes were on him with a gentle, concerned expression. "You look tired, Denny. Been up all night?"

"Just about, and we had a long hike with packs that weigh a ton apiece."

"You're not planning to go out on Opeongo, are you?"

Denny sighed and jerked his thumb toward Rick who was walking along the shore beside the docks. "*He* wants to."

Jack shook his head. "Opeongo doesn't look like much of a lake from here. This is Sproule Bay, but ahead it widens out and it goes on and on to the north. The wind gets a long sweep with nothing to stop it. It's a bad lake in a storm. Better wait till the weather clears."

"I'll tell my stepbrother." Denny pointed to the woodcarving that Jack was holding loosely in his hand. "What're you making?"

Jack held it up. "What do you think?"

The carving was not finished, but there was no mistaking the long nose and big ears.

Denny answered, "A wolf! Man," he said thoughtfully, "I sure like wolves now that I've gotten to know about them. Last night I howled and a pack of them answered me."

Jack nodded his pleasure. "The wolf's a noble animal. Doesn't deserve his bad reputation."

Denny heard a car drive up in front of the store. A moment later came a rattle of keys and the sound of a door being opened.

"I'd better go. I'm glad I met you," he said. Then he paused a moment longer, not wanting to leave this new friend. "Do you do woodcarving for a living?"

"No, I whittle for my own amusement. Oh, I sell some of my carvings, but I pay my bills by guiding fishermen."

The phone was on the wall inside the store with the phone book dangling from a chain beside it. Denny looked up the number of the provincial police and fished coins from his pocket. A moment later he was talking to a police officer at the station in Whitney, a town close to the eastern border of the park.

"I want to report an escaped criminal from the United States," he blurted out. Then he went on to describe Leach and to tell how he had smashed the Volkswagen windshield.

"We've already been notified we should watch for him," said the officer. "Does this man know where you are?"

"I don't think so. But he's looking for us."

"You stay there at the Opeongo dock and I'll send a car out to pick you up. We'll help you get your car to a garage."

"Thank you," said Denny. "But I don't think my stepbrother will wait. He wants to go out on Opeongo."

Rick was on the dock beside a green canoe he had rented. Its name was painted in bold white letters on the bow — *RAVEN*. The packs were already lashed in place.

When Denny relayed the police officer's message, Rick said, "You stay if you want to but Leach is too close to suit me. He may get here before the police. Or he might find me while I'm waiting for the car to get fixed."

Denny looked longingly toward the comfort of the rocking chairs on the porch of the store. His aching muscles urged him to sit there and wait. He was sure the police would arrange a way for him to get back to Buffalo.

Then his eyes turned to his stepbrother's sagging shoulders. How could he go home without Rick? His mother and Vince would think he had deserted him. Sure Rick was acting crazy, but all the more reason to stay with him.

Besides, it was really his fault that Leach

knew where to look for Rick. If only he hadn't written that note to Aunt Wilma!

"I'll go with you," he said. As he looked at the canoe bobbing gently in the water beside the dock, he admitted to himself that he wasn't going only because of Rick. He wanted to go. He wanted to see what it was like at the far end of Opeongo and beyond.

"Good." Rick gave him a friendly glance. "Into the bow, mate."

Denny warmed under Rick's approval. At once he felt less annoyed with him.

"What's in the bag?" asked Rick.

"Doughnuts. I bought them in the store. Want some?"

"I'll say."

Jack came down the slope as they pulled away from the dock. "Hey, there, *Raven*!" he called. "Get to shore when the wind comes up. You may need those life preservers you're wearing!"

The surface of Sproule Bay was smooth, but the sky was overcast and in the west dark clouds were gathering.

As soon as they left Sproule Bay, the water became choppy. But Denny was not prepared for the suddenness with which the storm hit.

A black cloud swooped over fast and low,

so low it seemed he could reach up and touch it. With it came winds that blew in furious gusts.

"Head for the left shore!" shouted Rick.

That meant fighting the wind, but Denny saw that Rick was right. Close to the west shore they would be protected from the wind — if they could get there.

A flash of lightning split the sky almost overhead, followed at once by thunder.

Denny forgot that he was tired, and paddled for his life. This was no place to be in a thunderstorm. On the water they were the highest objects around, which made them prime targets for lightning.

Then the rain came in a great downpour. It flattened their hair and ran down their necks. In a few seconds their clothes were soaked through and they were shivering with the cold. Where had the heat gone in such a hurry?

The water was collecting in the bottom of the *Raven*, but neither Denny nor Rick could take time to bail. As they headed at an angle toward the western shore, the canoe cut into foam-topped waves that tossed them as if they had no weight. Denny expected at any minute to be turned over.

"We'll land on the point!" shouted Rick.

Denny lifted his head and saw the arm of land reaching into the lake. It was flat and had a number of pine trees that were thrashing in the wind.

We're going to make it, after all, thought Denny. But at that moment a wave caught them broadside. The force of it tipped the canoe and flung both boys into the water.

Overboard

Denny was caught off guard, but he instinctively held his breath as he hit the water.

To his surprise, the lake water felt warm to his cold body. Although it closed over his head, his life jacket brought him bobbing to the surface.

The *Raven* was still upright, more than

half full of water. The packs were in place.
Denny clung to the side of the canoe and
pushed back his dripping hair.

The first thing he saw was the bag of
doughnuts floating nearby. He snatched it up
and laid it in the canoe on top of the packs.

Rick appeared only a few feet away and
swam to the canoe. His black hair was plas-
tered against his head.

"I lost my paddle," he said.

Denny looked around in surprise. "So did
I."

Neither paddle was in sight. They couldn't
be far away, but the rain was falling so heav-
ily he could see only three or four feet beyond
the canoe.

"Why don't you start for shore with the
canoe?" suggested Rick. "I'll see if I can find
the paddles."

He pulled off his sneakers and pants and
dumped them into the canoe. Then he swam
away and disappeared into the storm.

Denny, too, removed his sneakers. Seizing
the bow of the canoe, he started in what he
hoped was the direction of the shore. A few
minutes later he felt the wind slacken. Looking ahead, he saw the tops of tall trees lash-
ing back and forth as if shaken by an invisi-
ble monster. Waves foamed onto the narrow.

beach. To the right a thin arm of land jutted into the water.

The canoe began to move forward more easily; Denny discovered Rick had caught up with him and was pushing from the stern. He had found one of the paddles.

By the time they reached shore, the rain was slackening. After lifting the soggy packs onto the shore, the boys dumped the water from the canoe.

Suddenly Denny thought of his wallet. In a panic he reached for it. To his relief it was still safe in his hip pocket.

"Now what do we do?" he demanded, as he tied on his sneakers. "I'm frozen!"

"Me, too." Rick pointed to the arm of land two hundred feet to the north. "That looks like a camping spot. We might find a shelter over there where we can change to dry clothes."

Denny snatched up a pack and started toward the peninsula.

"Hold it!" shouted Rick. "Let's take the *Raven*. I want it where I can keep an eye on it. I don't want Leach pounding holes in it." He tossed the other pack and the food bag into the canoe. "Put your pack in and grab the other end."

Denny came back slowly. He had never in

his life been so cold and miserable, and as usual all Rick could do was think about Leach.

They set the canoe on the shore near a picnic table that stood under the tall pines on the peninsula. A path led all the way from the point into the woods.

"The shelter must be up this way," said Rick, turning inland. "Come on. Leave the food bag in the canoe."

Denny noticed that water was trickling from the food bag through the hole torn by the bear. He wondered if all the dried foods would start to swell up.

The path wound upward, but encouraged by a sign that said SHELTER, the boys toiled on. Halfway up the hill they found a lean-to with wooden bunks and a table.

Nothing in the packs was completely dry except Denny's camera, safe in its own plastic case. The sleeping bags were soaked.

Denny rubbed himself with a damp towel and pulled on a T-shirt and dungarees that were only slightly drier than the ones he had taken off. Although he had stopped shivering now that he was out of the wind, he was still cold.

"Now what?" he demanded.

"The rain has quit." Rick slid his arms into

a red flannel shirt. "I'm going to take the canoe and look around for the other paddle."

"Then what?"

"We'll go on, of course."

Denny was cold and hungry and out of patience with Rick. "Don't bother to look for the other paddle," he said abruptly. "You'll only need one. I'm not going with you."

"Don't be foolish. You can't stay here."

"You can take me back to the dock."

Rick faced him angrily. "I can't go back there! What do you want to do, lead me straight to Leach?"

"You're safer there than you will be if you go on. At least there are other people at the dock. The police may be there by now." He glared at Rick. "No matter what you do, I'm going home. I'll find someone to give me a lift to Huntsville and I can catch a bus there." He felt again for the comforting bulge of his wallet.

Rick taunted him. "You can't take it. You got dumped in the water so you're running home."

This was the last straw. Denny snatched up his wet dungarees. "If that's the way it looks to you, OK." He was so angry his voice shook. He sent the contents of the packs flying in all directions as he rummaged among them for his clothes.

"I've stuck with you long enough!" he raged. "Now you want me to spend the night in a wet sleeping bag and eat soggy food. No way!"

Rick watched him as if he were a new species of animal. "All right. Maybe it's better for you to go back. You can ride with me until we meet up with a boat that's headed for the dock."

Denny stuffed his clothes and camera into one of the extra plastic bags. "I'm going down," he said stiffly, "and see if there's anything fit to eat in that food bag. If a boat comes along I may catch a ride before you get there."

Rick said calmly, "Suit yourself."

Denny left the lean-to without a backward look.

As he took the muddy path down the hill, the future looked bleak. He dreaded going home to the empty house and Aunt Wilma's questions. But traveling on with Rick day after day, jumping at every noise and shadow, was even worse. Now with the food probably ruined and the sleeping bags wet, camping would be misery.

Rick should've put the packs into those plastic bags, he thought resentfully. Especially the food bag with that hole in it. But no, he was in too much of a hurry!

To Denny the worst part of all was losing his admiration for Rick. He had thought he had a brother to look up to, but how could he respect someone who lost his head and ran scared all the time?

When he reached the bottom of the hill, Denny decided not to take anything out of the food bag. He wasn't going to have Rick say he had used up any of his supplies.

But he was so hungry his stomach hurt all the way to his backbone. The doughnuts! They would solve that problem.

The white bag of doughnuts was not in the canoe. Had they left it on the beach where they landed?

Denny put his sack of clothes into the canoe and trudged wearily down the shore, searching all the way for the paper bag. At last he found it, lying on the gravelly sand close to the edge of the woods. The bag was wet, but the top was twisted shut, and to his delight, the doughnuts were in fair condition. He promptly sat down on the sand and leaned against a tree to enjoy his breakfast. The bright sunshine took the dampness out of his clothes and warmed him through.

He was finishing his third doughnut when he heard the sound of a motorboat approaching quickly from the south. It would do him no good. He needed to flag down someone going toward the dock.

However, he continued to watch as the boat drew nearer. To his surprise, it headed directly toward the spot where he and Rick had left the *Raven*.

As the boat came closer to the shore, Denny started to his feet, intending to wave, but he checked himself midway. The man who was running the motor had a hat pulled low over his eyes, so Denny could not see what he looked like.

But even at this distance, there was something familiar about the lone passenger who was scanning the shore with a pair of binoculars. Since he was hatless, Denny could see the shape of his head and his short blond hair.

Without taking his eyes from the boat, Denny inched back into the edge of the woods.

The boat, a red one like those he had seen at the boat rental station, nosed onto the beach and the passenger leaped out. Now Denny had no doubt who it was. Only Leach moved that way, like a boxer balanced on the balls of his feet, ready to dance in and jab.

Leach peered at the canoe, then strode back to the boat. He reached into his pocket for something which he handed to the man with the hat. After that he pushed the boat off the shore.

The boat backed away and turned toward the open lake. Leach took a quick look up and down the shore; he glanced the length of the peninsula. Any minute now he'd go up the path to the lean-to.

In Debt to the Wolf

That Leach! thought Denny. He was like a bloodhound.

He wondered if Rick had heard the motorboat. If Leach caught him off guard in the lean-to, he would not be able to escape.

Denny scrambled to his feet. Somehow he must warn Rick before Leach found him. His only hope was to cut diagonally through the woods to the lean-to, but he doubted if he had time.

Dropping the bag of doughnuts, he began to hurry among the trees with his hands outstretched before him to ward off branches. In spite of his care, his toe caught on a root and he fell into a thorny bush. As he scrambled to his feet and rushed on, it went through his mind that only a few minutes before he had hated Rick and now he was trying to save his life.

Well, I may be disappointed in him, he thought, but I don't want him killed.

He strained his eyes ahead. Yes, there was the little hill where the lean-to stood. But even as he looked, he caught a far-off glimpse of Rick's red shirt. He was on the way down the path. Denny knew there was no hope of reaching him before he met Leach. Travel through the woods was too slow.

Denny drew in a deep breath and then shouted as loud as he could, "Rick! Leach is coming!"

The red shirt moved on down the path. Apparently Rick was too far away to hear.

Denny gave one more shout, and pushed back toward the beach. In the open where he could make better time he might be able to overtake Leach before he met Rick. Though how could he stop Leach if he did catch up with him?

When Denny arrived at the shore, Leach was no place to be seen. That meant he was already on the path.

Denny dug in his toes and sprinted up the beach at the edge of the woods where the ground was firmest. Already tired from his long night of travel from Fork Lake, he was not in top form. His breath came quickly and his chest ached, but he ran as fast as he could.

Out of the corner of his eye, he saw to his surprise that the motorboat that had brought Rick's enemy was still in the bay. Was it waiting to take Leach away after he had settled his grudge?

Denny came abreast of the canoe and still he could hear no sound from Rick or Leach. He had a sick fear that Leach had already buried his knife in Rick's chest as he had done with Frank.

The path was just ahead. Denny slackened his speed and turned onto it. To his dismay only a few yards ahead of him Rick and Leach were facing each other like a pair of wrestlers.

Ducking behind a bush, Denny paused to take in the situation. Leach had his back toward him. His arms were outstretched on

162

either side and in his right hand was a knife with a thin, evil-looking blade.

Though Rick was facing Denny he gave no sign that he had seen him. All of his attention seemed to be on Leach. With his feet widespread, he moved slightly to the right and then to the left, as if watching for an opening so he could pitch into his opponent. There was a dark, wet stain on the right sleeve of his red shirt.

He's stopped running, thought Denny.

Leach made a quick motion with his right hand and Rick leaped aside.

"Got you jumping!" Leach said with a laugh. He crouched like a huge cat preparing to spring.

Denny realized he could not afford to wait for exactly the right moment. Leach might pounce any time now.

Denny stood up and stepped into the open. Rick's eyes flickered toward him and at the same time he started talking to Leach. The sound of his voice covered Denny's footsteps as he charged up the path and dived at Leach's legs in his best football tackle.

Leach, caught by surprise, toppled forward onto the muddy path. Rick flung himself onto his back while Denny clutched his legs.

"Got him!" panted Denny.

But Leach was not so easily defeated. Like a Gulliver tormented by tiny people, he gave a powerful kick that sent Denny sprawling. Rick still clung to his opponent, but he could not seem to capture the knife which Leach was swinging at him.

Denny realized he and Rick were no match for Leach and his knife. They might hold him off a few moments more, but the end was sure.

As Denny scrambled to his feet, he caught sight of a man coming up the path behind him. In spite of the battered straw hat he was wearing, Denny recognized Jack, the Indian guide he had met behind the store at the Opeongo dock.

He was the man in the motorboat, the one who had brought Leach here! Would he be on Leach's side now?

At least I can try, thought Denny. He shouted, "Jack! Help us! He's trying to kill my brother!"

He didn't wait for the guide's answer, but ran back to pounce on Leach's feet. This time Leach twisted around and sliced at him with the knife. Denny felt the blade on the back of his neck like a hot iron. Surprised, he released his hold and clutched his neck.

A lean figure raced past him and seized Leach's right arm. Within seconds the knife was in Jack's hand and he was standing over Leach and Rick.

"Get up, you!" he roared. When Leach did not obey, he lifted him by the collar.

Rick rolled clear and stared in surprise at the newcomer.

Jack pointed to Rick. "You got some rope?"

Rick nodded. "Tent ropes."

"Tie him up!"

Denny tore open the pack that lay on the ground where Rick had dropped it. He handed the rope to his stepbrother.

Leach fought savagely against being tied until Jack landed a blow under his chin. After that he seemed groggy.

Denny watched with satisfaction as Leach's hands were tied behind his back and his feet were hobbled so he could take only short steps.

The guide jerked his head toward Denny. "Get your gear. We're ready to go."

They tied the canoe, loaded with the packs, to the rear of the boat. With a combination of pushing and threats, Jack maneuvered a still shaky Leach into the boat where he made him lie down on the bottom.

Then with Rick operating the motor and

Jack at Leach's head and Denny at his feet, they set off for the Opeongo dock.

"Hey, Jack! How come you brought Leach out here?" Denny had to raise his voice over the noise of the motor.

"He said he was trying to catch up with some friends to go camping with them." Jack shrugged. "Happens all the time. By his description I knew he was looking for you two. He came maybe ten minutes after you left, but I wouldn't start out till the storm was over."

"How'd you know where to find us?" asked Rick.

"Wasn't easy. I kept looking all along the west shore. I didn't think you'd get as far as you did."

"But you came right to the place where we were and you couldn't see either of us," said Denny.

"Yeah, but we saw your canoe, the *Raven*. All the rental boats have names. And Leach, here, had some binoculars."

Denny was still puzzled. "You didn't go away after you dropped off Leach. Why was that?"

"I had a feeling something was wrong," said Jack. "For one thing, he didn't have any pack. Then he gave me a big tip. Too big. I was sitting there off shore wondering what to do when I saw you run down the beach like you had a bear on your tail. So I came to shore to see what was going on."

Leach was losing his groggy look. Denny, seeing the hatred in the man's eyes, was thankful for the ropes that bound his hands and feet.

Jack reached into his pocket and pulled out the carving on which he had been working that morning.

"Here." He tossed it to Denny. "Here's a wolf for you."

Denny turned it over, admiring the fine work. The wolf was lying like a dog with his paws in front of him and his head alert.

"I'll always keep it," he promised.

"Wolves!" grunted Leach unexpectedly. "I would've caught up with you last night on that island if it hadn't been for those wolves."

Rick turned sharply to Leach. "You heard the wolves howling? So did we."

Leach did not answer, but Rick persisted. "Did you go to Fork Lake early this morning? Or did you see our canoe in the bog?"

Leach's eyes burned into Rick's. He spat out his reply. "I'll get you yet!"

The howling must have given Leach a bad scare, thought Denny. Maybe it had sounded louder near the road. Funny that a tough guy like that would be afraid of wolves. He must've read those old stories about wolves in Russia killing people and eating them.

Denny clutched his carving more tightly. Now he owed another debt to the wolves.

Halfway to the Opeongo dock they met another boat that flagged them down. In it were two members of the provincial police.

When they pulled close and saw Leach in the bottom of the boat, one of the officers remarked, "You've done our work for us, I see. We'd have been here sooner, but that storm blew a tree down across the road."

The other policeman said, "Looks as if two of you need first aid."

"Mine's just a scratch." Denny touched his neck with careful fingers.

Rick looked down at the wet stain on his sleeve as if surprised to see the blood. "Nothing serious," he assured the police.

The officer released his hold on the red boat. "We'll escort you back to the dock."

Two hours later, Rick and Denny were back at Mew Lake in their old camping spot.

Leach was on the way to the United States, and Rick's car was at the garage in Whitney.

Denny was hanging his sleeping bag on a line to dry when he saw the Adams' car drive in beside their trailer. He was alone because Rick had gone out to phone Aunt Wilma and Beth.

The entire Adams family climbed out of their car. Holly was the first to notice that there was a tent in the camping place beside the lake. She came slowly down the road until she saw Denny. Then she broke into a run.

That night as Rick and Denny lay in their tent, wrapped in blankets provided by Mrs. Adams, Rick said, "I was thinking, Denny. Leach would have finished me off today if it weren't for you. Thanks for pitching in to help me."

"But Leach wouldn't have come to Algonquin in the first place if I hadn't left that note."

"Oh, that!" Rick dismissed the note. "Leach would've found me, anyway. You saw how he operates."

"He said he'd get you yet," Denny reminded him. "Are you worried about that?"

"No. Well, not much. He'll be in prison a

long time. And anyway, I found out today I wasn't as scared when I was fighting him as I was all the time I was on the run."

"You were great!" Denny said admiringly. "Would you do it again?" he asked.

"What?"

"Would you tell on Leach and be a witness against him?"

"Yes, I would." Rick spoke with conviction. "A man like Leach would go on killing. Another person's life doesn't mean anything to him. You can't let a man like that roam free."

They lay in silence. Outside the tent Denny could hear the *chunk* of frogs and the faint music of a guitar being played at the far end of the campground.

He was almost asleep when Rick's voice came out of the darkness beside him.

"By the way, Denny," he said, "when you asked Jack for help, you said, 'He's killing my *brother*.'"

"I forgot to say stepbrother," admitted Denny.

Rick said quietly, "I hope you'll keep on forgetting."